THE GINGERBREAD WOMAN

The
Gingerbread Woman

Jennifer Johnston

Copyright © 2000 Jennifer Johnston

The right of Jennifer Johnston to be identified as the Author of
the Work has been asserted by her in accordance with the
Copyright, Designs and Patents Act 1988.

First published in 2000
by REVIEW

An imprint of Headline Book Publishing

10 9 8 7 6 5 4 3 2 1

ISBN 0 7472 2137 5

Typeset by Avon Dataset Ltd, Bidford-on-Avon, Warks

Printed and bound in Great Britain by
Clays Ltd, St Ives plc.

Headline Book Publishing
A division of Hodder Headline
338 Euston Road
London NW1 3BH

www.reviewbooks.co.uk
www.hodderheadline.com

For Pat, the treasure,
with much love

Der Frühling will kommen
der Frühling meine Freud';
nun mach'ich mich fertig,
zum Wandern bereit.

Spring is on its way
Springtime – my delight!
Now I shall make ready
To begin my travels . . .

Der Hirt auf dem Felsen (The Shepherd on the Rock)
Wilhelm Müller (1794–1824),
set to music by Franz Schubert

My mother makes jam.

Seasonal jam.

Raspberry, blackberry and apple, loganberry, marrow and ginger, golden crab-apple jelly and, of course, marmalade.

Not a million miles from here – just down the road, in fact, across the railway line and turn right.

Five minutes' walk.

She makes other things too: shortbread biscuits, sponge cakes, rich fruit cake, brandy snaps . . . could go on for ever, but where's the point. I'm sure you get the message.

There is no one left in the house now for whom to make jam, but she continues to do it as she has always done. And we, her four children, mark the seasons, winter, spring, summer, autumn, by our dogged and grateful acceptance of the jewel-coloured jars that she packs neatly into cardboard boxes and hands to us as we leave her house after our brief familial visits.

'The jam, dear,' she will say. 'Don't forget the raspberry jam. I know the children like it even if you don't.'

She is right, of course. The children love it; and they love the sponge cakes filled with rich chocolate cream and the gingerbread men.

'Run, run, as fast as you can, you can't catch me, I'm the gingerbread man.'

They think she's slightly dotty when she says that to them. They prefer deadly war games or other adventures on their computer screens to stories about foxes and silly little gingerbread men.

I have to admit that I love the gingerbread men too; their slightly cinnamon taste and their chewy texture. She knows this, remembers it from long ago, and though I don't have any children for her to indulge, she indulges this childishness in me happily. None of us have to worry about her yet; she is hale and hearty and fully in control of her life and, she thinks, of ours. We let her think that, but in reality we get on with what we have to do and don't run to her as we used to with the grown-up equivalents of cut knees and broken hearts.

I didn't choose to live round the corner from her, in the way that I do; my little house was left to me by an aunt and though I haven't spent much time in it, except for recent months, I have never mustered up the energy to sell it. It has become a sort of repository for my bits and pieces – old clothes, childhood's books that I could never bear to give to my nephews and nieces, other oddments that I have collected on my travels – and at this moment I have become a temporary part of this consoling mess.

I am by way of being the cosmopolitan one in the family. I have lived and earned my living in London, Paris, briefly, and New York and am seriously contemplating having a look at Sydney when i recover my full strength and energy. As you may gather, I am not an adventurous person. i don't go looking for danger, I just like to get out of this cage away from the jam and the familial duties, both of which i love and hate at the same time.

I suppose I should tell you at this moment how i earn my keep, how I manage to wander as I have done around the world – not that it matters all that much, but people, you people always want to know so much irrelevant stuff. *What?* you ask? *How? Why? When exactly did this happen? What was her motivation? Who? Whom? Whither?* All those wonderful w.h. words that only we, the Irish, can pronounce properly. Writers tell you as much as they wish – that should be enough for you, but it seldom is. Anyway, i'm not really a writer; I always thought that I would like to be a poet. I would like to be able to write stuff like Roger McGough.

> *They don't fuck you up, your mum and dad*
> *(Despite what Larkin says)*
> *It's other grown-ups, other kids*
> *Who, in their various ways*
>
> *Die. And their dying casts a shadow*
> *Numbering all our days*
> *And we try to keep from going mad*
> *In multifarious ways.*
>
> *And most of us succeed, thank God,*
> *So if, to coin a phrase,*
> *You're fucked up, don't blame your mum and dad*
> *(Despite what Larkin says).*

Yes. I like the notion of a poem ending with a bracket. I also like to laugh from time to time. This sort of stuff makes me laugh. Not Larkin, I do have to say. Not Larkin.

I went briefly several years ago to an analyst – that was during my spell in London – and he tried to persuade me that i wanted to sleep with my father and somehow exterminate my mother. I found this quite confusing, so i stopped going to see him. No harm to my father, but i had seen sexier men around, I had actually lusted after and been to bed with younger and sexier men. I had no problems in that area of my life. Then I told him about my mother's jam, and how I would be bereft without that but he didn't believe me. Analysts don't really care about things like jam. Roger McGough seemed more helpful and indubitably less expensive.

i am digressing . . . by the way, you may have noticed that I am having problems with some of the upper-case Is. I'm sorry about this. It has happened to me since my operation and I think has something to do with loss of self-esteem. Please bear with me.

Where was i . . . ? About to tell you how I earn my living. I do odd jobs for newspapers – write book reviews, features on entertaining topics, arty pieces and interviews with reasonably famous people . . . *not* film stars. i draw the line at film stars. My main source of income though is lecturing. I am by profession a lecturer in Modern Irish Literature. Not Synge, Yeats or Joyce. That's a mug's game; that's big business these days, something I have no head for at all. I took a year's sabbatical from Trinity College several years ago and got a taste for the roving life. I discovered that the world is full of universities delighted to give me a year's work talking to their students about Elizabeth Bowen, John McGahern, Edna O'Brien, Francis Stewart, Aidan Higgins, John Banville, Sean O'Faoilean . . . the list is endless and growing every day. I stick with prose writers: talking about poetry to an ocean of undergraduates makes me feel ill in the head. And i bring things home from my travels and stack them round the walls of my little house here in Dalkey. Centre of the World. Then I come here to lick my wounds and eat my mother's jam, take big deep breaths and get ready to go away again.

At this moment in my life I listen to a lot of music, i sing in the bath and the kitchen, i read books by writers who are younger than I am; sometimes I find it quite difficult to breathe and the doctor has told me not to lift heavy weights or laugh too hard. I don't really see much around me to laugh about, and yet I have always needed to laugh. Someone, some Irish writer but stupidly i can't put a name on him at this moment, said, 'Take away this cursed gift of laughter and give us tears instead.' He was right, of course. Laughter *is* one of our curses in this country. Great roaring jeering laughter, titters behind the hand, satire, mischief, savage little jokes. We don't seem to be able to manage without any of that. Anyway i have to manage for another few weeks or my stomach may burst open and all sorts of horrible things fall out.

I walk each day, quite gently up here to the top of Killiney Hill and sit in the sun by the obelisk watching the mothers with prams and the toddlers running over the grass and the real walkers striding out, their hips swinging satisfactorily from side to side. Soon i will be fit enough to do that too and then I won't want to do it; i will want to go to Sydney or Ascension Island or Anchorage – now there's a name to conjure with. I will take my abilities with me and when I come home, for indubitably, this will always be home, I will bring with me more odds and ends and stack them neatly round the walls of my house.

One day when I come back i won't be able to open the door. 'Too much rubbish in there, dear,' my mother will say. 'There's not even room for a pound of jam.' Then I suppose I will give up travelling, or running or whatever it is that I am doing and stay at home.

Below me today the sea is a startling silver colour; in fact, it hurts my eyes to look at it for more than a moment or two. Like a huge animal it crawls with white lines of foam moving across its wrinkled back. Then i shut my eyes. I feel the touch of the sun's April warmth and then the cutting edge of the bloody east wind blowing from God knows where; the Steppes of Russia we have always been told, but I make a point of not believing everything that people say to me. I could stand here with my eyes shut for a long time, if it weren't for the east wind. It carves through my clothes and presses its knife edge against the scars, the visible signs of my mutilation. I pull my coat around me. I listen to the sounds of normal life behind me; the calls of mothers to their children, the barking of dogs, and the brisk thudding along the path of the occasional jogger.

At such moments in the last few months I have sometimes become engulfed in a frightening fog of self-pity. i really hate this. I have never intended to be that sort of person. I have always tried to be well balanced, resilient – cool, they call it now. Self-pity is not cool.

I did speak to my doctor about this.

He laughed. He is an old family friend, so he has the right to laugh. 'For heaven's sake, Clara, you are post-operative. Give yourself a chance.'

He then wrote something on my case notes; probably a memo to himself, for future use. *Remember to send Clara to a shrink if she carries on like this.* Maybe not, of course.

He then repeated what he had already said. 'Give yourself a chance.'

I am doing just that.

Now when I feel the edges of my mind beginning to mist over with despair I fill my head with music. I sing – mainly in my head, but sometimes also aloud. I conjure up such singers as Callas, Jessye Norman, Kathleen Ferrier – I give them the acoustic in my head and let them rip.

I open my eyes again and stare into the wind and then down the coast past Bray Head to the little snout of Greystones leaning into the sea. The wind buffets me, quite gently. It is veering now to the south, not so disagreeable any more and inside me the voice of Benita Valente sings with a charm that at this moment I find very seductive.

> *Wenn auf dem höchsten Fels ich steh',*
> *In's tiefe Tal herniederseh',*
> *Und singe:*

German was never one of my best subjects.

In fact, to be perfectly honest it wasn't one of my subjects at all.

I sing along inside my head.

'*Fern aus dem tiefen, dunkeln Thal . . .*'

It is not one of the world's most beautiful languages. It's not a happy language, like Italian; nor a romantic language, like Russian, or indeed my own unspoken language, Irish, both full of soft curvaceous sounds that embrace you, invite you to listen. German halts you in your tracks. *Stop right there*, it seems to say. *Do not come one step nearer.*

'. . . *schwingt sich empor der Wiederhall.*'

It sings well though.

I sing well in my head.

'*Der Wiederhall der Klüfte.*'

On the edge.

I stand here right on the edge and sing.

'*Und singe . . .*'

I like the feel of the land dropping steeply away below me, the narrow road and then the railway tracks and beyond them the shining sea.

A bird's-eye view.

'Hello there.'

'*Je weiter meine Stimmer dringt,*
je heller sie mir wiederklingt von unten . . .'

'Miss, ah . . . excuse me. Hello?'

I ignore such invasive voices.

Und singe.

* * *

He hadn't thought to bring his coat.

The sun and the blue sky had beckoned him out from his bedroom in the hotel where he had spent the last week, and for the first time he had snatched up the dog's lead from the table by the door and gone out without putting on his coat. Now the wind found its way through his jeans and sweatshirt and made him shiver. Made him swear too about his own stupidity.

Pansy was happy though and thumped her tail against his leg as he walked up the road towards the park. She was even happier when he bent down just inside the park gates and released her; she was away off at once into the trees, her nose to the ground snuffling and searching for some exciting scent.

She was not made uneasy by the unfamiliarity of her surroundings; from time to time she would look back towards him just to check that he had not disappeared, her tail would flick for a moment and then she would continue with her search.

Faithless creature!

He smiled a sour little smile and two children ran past him, calling to a woman who pushed a buggy up the hill in front of him. They were breathless with laughter.

'Mammy, Mammy,' one of them called. 'Wudja hang on a minute. You're going too fast.' Obediently the woman stopped walking. She turned and waited, smiling at the children as they scrambled towards her.

Laurence began to shake; his whole body was struck with what seemed to be an ague. He couldn't move, couldn't put one foot in front of the other, he could only stand trembling, his arms wrapped tightly across his chest in an effort not to fall apart. The woman with the pram looked in his direction for a moment and then turned and went on her way up the hill, the children chattering beside her.

He had no idea how long he stood there; it was Pansy gently

nudging at his leg that brought him back to reality.

'Yes, girl.' He touched her head with a finger. He began to walk again and Pansy, for a few moments, walked sedately beside him.

The sunlight flickered down through the tall trees, just starting to come into leaf.

I thought I had left all that behind me.

Legs move, in out, scuffed old suede slip-ons, in and out. In, out. I would like to run. I would like to come out into the sun, out of this green trembling light. I would like to burn up in the sun, self-destruct. I would like to explode.

Explode. Echoes of explosion carrying on the wind, the smell of exploding flesh floating with the echoes. I carry that smell in my nose. In there with my hatred, the smell of exploding flesh.

All my imagination, of course. I have never seen flesh exploding, only in my mind's eye. Tender flesh.

Snap out of it, Lar.

They'll be coming for you one day, the men in white coats. The men with the needles and the straitjackets and the bottles of liquid that take away the pain, if you don't snap out of it. That's what people say anyway.

'It's time you snapped out of it, Lar. Aye it is. Well beyond time.'

His father's tired face as Lar had opened the front door to him; eyes drooping at the corners, faded blue now and full of sadness and at the same time a curious anger.

'You must listen to me. You've got to snap out of it, son.'

And he had slammed the door in the old man's face.

The paint on the inside of the door was losing its whiteness now; he had stared at it, stared through it at his father's stooped figure on the other side.

The door needs painting, he had thought and turned and walked back into the kitchen. He heard the creak and slam of the garden gate as his father had stepped out onto the street, squaring his shoulders, sticking out his chin, swinging his walking stick with bravado. Such bloody bravado.

Legs move, in out.

His father's face melted into the trees and a small cloud passed across the sun and created for a few moments shade where before there had been light.

I must send them a postcard.

Mum and Dad.

I must let them know that I am alive.

Here, in Dublin.

City of their dreams.

Don't worry, I will write on it. I'm all right. Sorry. Will I write sorry? No, definitely not. X.O. Lar. I will do that, later today. I will find a suitable card. Picture of The Four Courts? Trinity College? Panoramic view of Dublin Bay? City of their dreams. Wish you were here. No, I won't write that either.

Such thoughts brought him out into the windy sunshine; children kicked footballs and women held their hair and chatted to acquaintances, the sound of their voices fluttered and swooped like birds on the wind.

He walked past them up towards the obelisk and then turned and looked out towards the sea.

He never had any desire to go to the edge and look down.

'Why can't I fly?' he had once asked his father. Dad had smiled at him and launched as was his wont into a long dissertation on aerodynamics. Laurence was none the wiser at the end and his fear of heights had remained the same.

That woman was there again.

It was the third time he had noticed her standing on the edge like that, her dark coat flapping in the wind, as if indeed her father had never lectured her on aerodynamics and she was about to take off across the bay. He had noticed how thin she was, and pale like a ghost.

Maybe she was a ghost. Maybe she could fly.

Her eyes were fixed each time he had seen her on the horizon, but he knew that they weren't seeing the seascape there in front of her. She took a small step even closer to the edge and he began to run towards her.

'Hello there!'

She didn't seem to hear but moved her hands sideways in an awkward gesture as if she were addressing someone.

He slowed down as he got close to her. Maybe he was being unutterably foolish. He felt his face becoming hot; he wanted to turn and go back up the hill, back to the path wandering through the trees, back to his hotel.

'Miss . . . ah . . . excuse me. Hello?'

She turned and looked at him. She frowned slightly as if he had interrupted some important thing that had been going on in her head.

'What is it?'

'I just wondered if you were all right.'

She looked puzzled.

'All right?'

'Yes. I just wondered. I do apologise for . . . You're so close to the edge and I . . . well I . . .'

She looked down at the ground, at the steep hill falling away below her, at the trees hiding the coast road, the roofs and then the railway line and beyond that, the sea. A bird surfed on the wind, rose and fell, its wings outstretched. It looked lazy, she thought, a drifter.

'I like the edge,' she said at last.

'I suffer from vertigo,' he said. 'I couldn't bear to stand so close.'

'I don't. I have no fear of heights.'

'I thought that perhaps . . .' He left the meaning hanging between them, buffeted by the south-east wind.

'No,' she said. 'I would never do a thing like that. I have thought of it from time to time, but rejected it as a solution.'

'I thought you might slip. You know, so close . . . the wind. You didn't seem to be looking.'

'I wouldn't slip.'

'Well, that's all right then.'

He turned and began to walk away. So much for showing a caring interest in human beings. He wondered where Pansy was.

'Thank you,' the woman called after him.

He nodded his head, but didn't turn back. No sign of that bloody dog.

'Pansy!' He let out a yell.

No answering bark.

He whistled. He wasn't much good at whistling. He had never been able to develop that really piercing tone that so many of his friends could produce. Something to do with the formation of his mouth, or the projection of his breath – hardly one of life's major problems.

He stopped and looked back at the woman. She had moved several steps back from the edge now and stood hunched into her coat looking after him.

✵ ✵ ✵

Und singe.

Und singe . . .

The words no longer echo.

Did he shout 'Pansy'?

I cannot believe he shouted 'Pansy'.

Now the music has gone and the echo. The clarinet is no longer hurling back from Bray Head.

Gone.

Blast this interloper, interferer, intervener in my life. I wonder, do i look like a potential suicide?

This is my best coat.

I don't think that I would commit suicide in my best coat. It would upset my mother. Anyway, any fool can see that you wouldn't jump off the top of Killiney Hill if you wanted to commit suicide. You'd probably just break a whole lot of bones and have to spend the rest of your life in a wheelchair. Motorised. I wonder how fast you can go in a motorised wheelchair?

I wonder, if i did commit suicide, what my mother would do with all my stuff? Divide it equally among my three siblings? Probably that. She is a woman of infinite fairness. 'One for you and one for you.' Pictures, knick-knacks, pots of jam. 'Pity about the best coat,' she might say. 'That would have suited Rosie. A lot of wear still in that coat. Expensive clothes last for ever.' She has never been aware of the fickleness of fashion.

Rosie, of course, would have rejected it out of hand. 'I don't want to look like a crow,' she would say. 'Clara always liked looking like a crow.' Caw, caw. I hope they might cry for a while and remember in the end all of my better points.

He thinks I'm staring at him.

I will smile and say something pleasant.

After all, he may have just saved my life.

☆   ☆   ☆

'Who is Pansy?'

The woman spoke after a long look in his direction.

He waved the lead. 'Dog.'

She laughed and then as if she were in pain grimaced and moved her right hand across her body protectively.

'What a crazy name for a dog.'

He didn't say anything. He had thought the same when Caitlin had smiled up at him, the squirming puppy in her arms.

'We'll call her Pansy.'

'Why on earth Pansy?'

'I just feel like calling her Pansy.' And at that moment the puppy had licked her face and she had laughed. 'Dear Pansy.'

Bugger.

He took a deep breath.

'There's no accounting for tastes,' he said.

The woman nodded. 'Actually I was listening to music.'

He heard Pansy's bark in the distance.

'Just standing there. I do that quite a lot. I listen.'

He saw the dog galloping towards him across the grass with some small child's ball in her mouth.

'To music.'

'Great. That's great,' he said, his eyes and his mind on Pansy and the possibility of an angry mother.

'So I wasn't . . . Is that Pansy?'

He nodded. The dog stopped about six feet away from him and wagged her tail. She carefully put the ball on the ground between her feet and looked down at it and then up at him. It was a red ball. It looked quite new.

'That's a good girl,' he said experimentally, and bent down to take the ball.

Quick as a flash she picked it up and moved away out of reach. She put the ball on the ground again and then sat beside it, tempting him to try again.

He did. She moved again. She gave a little bark. Laurence was aware of the woman's amused face.

'Pansy, please,' he said. He turned towards the woman. 'It's not her ball.'

'It is now.'

'Pansy!' Her tail thumped.

He took another little step; she retreated. Her eyes shone.

'Do you have to stand there and watch me?' he said irritably to the woman. 'You're making me feel very foolish.'

She put her hand into the pocket of her coat and took out a paper bag. Pansy once more evaded his grasping hand. A grey cloud blew in front of the sun.

'It's going to rain,' said the woman. 'Rain was forecast for this afternoon.'

'Why don't you go home, or . . . ?'

Pansy barked again.

Across the other side of the grass, women were gathering their children, perturbed by the signals in the sky.

'Or?'

'Well, at least go somewhere else.'

'I'm enjoying this. I don't get much entertainment at the moment. Who wins, dumb animal or . . .?'

'Dumb human?'

'You said it.'

She put her hand into the paper bag and took out a shortbread biscuit. She held it out towards him. 'Here?'

He shook his head.

'No thanks.'

'It's not for you, dumb human. It's . . .'

'Bribery?'

'Top of the class.'

A large raindrop burst on the side of his face.

Pansy barked.

The women were scurrying now for the shelter of the trees.

He took the biscuit from her. It looked really good, home-made, like his mother might make. He bent forward towards Pansy, holding the biscuit out.

'Good girl,' he said. 'Biccy.'

She left the ball unprotected and moved towards him. She sniffed like a connoisseur at the biscuit and then took it gently from his fingers.

'It's all quite simple really,' said the bloody know-all woman.

Laurence picked up the ball and looked at it. It was slimy and the air was seeping out of it through a hole made by Pansy's teeth.

'Oh God,' he said in disgust. He walked across the path and dropped the ball into a dustbin and then wiped his fingers on his trouser leg. 'You are a disgrace to doghood.'

Pansy wagged her tail.

'Just badly trained. It's not her fault.' The woman held the paper bag out towards Laurence again. 'Have one yourself,' she suggested.

'No thanks.'

'They're really good.'

He shook his head.

It was now raining quite hard. They appeared to be the only idiots left in the park.

'My mother made them.'

'No thanks.'

'Suit yourself. You don't know what you're missing. See you round.' She shoved a biscuit into her mouth and walked off chewing. Hopefully, Pansy ran after her.

'Pansy!' he yelled, and moved briskly away in the opposite direction, towards the shelter of the trees.

Listening to music! That was a rare one all right.

Caitlin had listened to music; real music, played fortissimo. He would hear it when he came from the school, raising the roof of her studio at the bottom of the garden. It was lucky, he often said to her, not being a music man himself, that they lived apart like they did, away from neighbours with sensitive ears or differing taste to hers.

She put her tongue out and carefully licked the end of her paintbrush, coaxing it with tongue and lips into a sharp point. She touched it into the paint and drew a clear thin line on the canvas, then she looked up and smiled at him.

'Five minutes,' she said. 'I will come up to the house in five minutes and then

you can fuck me and make me scream and no one will hear that either. There are great advantages to not living in a housing estate.'

Her words pattered out into silence as the raindrops fell through the leaves.

What is the point in all this?

This running away?

This pain?

They all tell you it dissipates.

'Life can become normal again,' they say. Even my old father believes that.

I always used to think he knew everything. Now I slam the door in his face and have to leave the country because I can't say sorry. *Won't* say sorry — that's what Mum would say. 'Who do you think you are, treating your daddy like that? Do you think you're the only person in the world has suffered tragedy? Look around you, son.' That's what she would have said if I hadn't run. Thrown some clothes and Pansy in the back of the car and driven off. I don't even remember locking the front door, now I come to think of it.

A cold wet nose nudged his hand.

'We'll be OK, Pansy. That's what they all say.'

He didn't believe it.

He bent down and fastened the lead to the dog's collar. They trudged together back the way they had come. The rain was unrelenting. There was no sign of the biscuit woman.

☆   ☆   ☆

Bloody good shortbread biscuits, Clara thought.

Discerning dog.

I'll have a long hot bath when I get home; wash my hair, turn on the record player fortissimo — drown out the sound of rain. I will contemplate my scar, still much too visible for my liking, in spite of the dollops of vitamin E i massage into my stomach every day.

'Suppose I had been a belly dancer?'

I'd asked the doctor that question before I came out of the hospital and he had laughed.

'Get away with you, woman,' he had said.

He then explained that, had he carried such thoughts about my life and career in his head, he, at great expense, could have found a surgeon who would have done a job of invisible mending second to none.

'At great expense,' he said again.

'Naturally,' I said to him.

We understood each other.

'Just take care, Clara.' He held my wrist in his cool fingers as he spoke. 'Don't laugh too much for a couple of weeks.'

To give him his due, he has kept his mouth buttoned; he has not told my mother the full and nasty truth as to why I had to undergo such butchery.

I wonder if I do stand on the edge in the hope that the wind will do for me the job that I am not prepared to do for myself. I hope not.

I don't think I have any desire to step or jump, or even fall out of life. The fact that I don't think much of it at the moment doesn't mean that there are no surprises left to come; even the simple pleasure of the early-morning smell of the distant sea through my bedroom window gives me a momentary nudge each morning. I am glad to be able to say that.

My mother, who is getting old and filled with anxieties, says that I shouldn't sleep with my bedroom window open; this is because I live in a cottage, and sleep on the ground floor and she believes implicitly that i will one night be murdered in my bed by some drug-crazed teenager. This fear, I think, sums up her attitude to modern life.

I often wonder if my mother was ever young. I have no recollection of girlishness in her at all, no giggles or flirtatiousness, no petulance; her passions have always seemed to be for order, harmony and a sort of family loyalty that from time to time makes me want to throw up. Her face and body have become lined and wrinkled, softened with age; she has grown smaller, even some of her grandchildren are now taller than she is, but her personality does not seem to have changed at all in all the years that I have known her. But then perhaps I have never really known her, just someone called mother.

I know she would like me to sell my cottage and move in with her. Sometimes she offers to send Patty, her cleaning lady, round to give my place a good going-over. I always refuse politely but firmly.

'I like it the way it is,' I say to her and she sighs.

'I rattle round in all those empty rooms,' she said to me just after I had come out of hospital.

'Sell it,' I advised. 'The way things are at the moment you'd get a fortune for it. Buy something smaller. Dumb down.' An expression she had never heard before.

'Nineteen fifty-two,' she said, 'was the year we moved in.'

'It's time to move on.'

'You could have two or three rooms of your own. We could make a nice little flat for you.'

'I have a nice little house.'

'I'm sure you don't eat properly.'

'Mother, I'm thirty-five.'

'Yes, dear. I know.'

Maybe I am being unkind. There is always the possibility that she needs me more than I feel I need her. Maybe she is afraid, lonely, without a purpose in life, except for making jam. Should I bear this vulnerability in mind?

Nah!

I feel I want to run a thousand miles.

But I can't run at this moment in time – or laugh, if it comes to that.

How many miles of gut is it that we have winding around inside us? Just imagine if it were to spill out here on the Killiney Hill Road.

It doesn't bear thinking about.

So I won't think about it.

I will walk slowly home and write a novel.

*　*　*

He didn't buy a postcard on his way back to the hotel.

Let them sweat, he thought.

He was sweating; his forehead was damp and he could feel a slow trickle moving down past his right ear towards his chin. And yet he wasn't warm. He should have brought his jacket.

How can I sweat and not be warm? That was the sort of silly question to which Caitlin would have known the answer. She had always known the answers to all his questions.

'I am the fount of all wisdom. I like to spew. I like the feeling that I am a walking encyclopaedia, a Thesaurus, a shedder of light into dark corners.'

She had looked at him for a moment and grinned. Sunlight came through the window and shone through her disordered hair.

'Or perhaps I am just a liar,' she said. 'We are all liars.'

'Yes,' he said. 'Oh, Caitlin. Caitlin.'

He unlocked the boot of the car and took out the dog's bowl. Pansy wagged her tail and then sat down to wait. He filled the bowl with dog nuts and put it on the ground in front of her. She sniffed cautiously at it for a moment and then began to eat. He bent down and scratched her head and then went to the tap at the other end of the car park to fetch her some water.

I'll give them a ring, he thought, that's what I'll do all right. He held his hand under the tap for a moment and then wiped his face. The water trickled over his chin and down his neck. And I'll go and have several pints in a pub – I haven't done that for a long time. Get a bit blotto . . . his father's neatly old-fashioned word, that. Then he wondered if he could take Pansy with him. Maybe they didn't let dogs into Dublin pubs. Maybe.

He put the bowl of water down beside the dog and leaned against the car. I am probably having a nervous breakdown, he thought. One bit of me wants to come out the other side and another bit wants me to stay like this for ever. Hurting. I'm afraid if I stop hurting that I will forget.

He smiled angrily.

Garbage, psychological garbage. We get it hurled at us from every direction – newspapers, airwaves, TV. Have you got a problem? Do you hurt? Are you alienated from society? Incapable of functioning on a normal level? Suicidal? Have you been mugged, or lost a loved one? Call your local health board or Dr Anthony Clare. Counselling is close at hand. The Seventh Cavalry is on the way. Tara tara.

'Woof,' said Pansy, full now of dog nuts.

The hotel was an ugly building, perched on the edge of the sea; a small island was just off the shore, lashed at this moment by wintry little waves. He remembered a sunny afternoon when he and Caitlin had gone over there and wandered round. The hillside had been covered with goats and they had found the smell quite disagreeable and they hadn't stayed long. Now rain danced in the puddles of the car park and the clouds seemed low enough to touch. Pansy sniffed around among the few cars until she found one that pleased her, then she squatted almost daintily beside it and shat.

Laurence opened the back of his car and called her. He put the two bowls inside and she jumped in after them. He closed the back.

'Seeya, doll,' he said, and flicked the car window with a fingernail.

His room did not look out over the grey flickering sea and the island of goats; nor the little harbour where the small boats clanked and clattered and where, from time to time, dispirited-looking men sold fish. It looked instead towards the road and the gently sloping hill with its scattering of houses, neatly clipped hedges and palm trees.

'*Who do they think they are,*' he had asked Caitlin, '*these people with their palm trees and their geraniums? You couldn't grow a palm tree in Ballycastle or Glenarm.*'

She giggled.

'Are we underprivileged in the northern part of this island because we can't grow palm trees? My mother would love to have geraniums ramping up the walls of her house.'

'Maybe there's a few people here who would rather have the ocean on their doorstep,' she said. 'Puffins, guillemots, cormorants. All that limitless fresh air.'

'Pretty unlikely.' He had become suddenly anxious. 'Would you like to live here? Prefer to . . .?'

She had taken his hand and held it gently to her cheek. 'I prefer the ocean to the Irish Sea. I prefer the cormorants to the geraniums.'

He took off his damp clothes and threw them into the corner of the room. Then he turned on the shower and stood under it as hot as he could bear it, scalding spears pricking into his skin. Wrapping himself in a towel, he lay down on the bed, a double bed of moderate comfort. The telephone was close to his right hand.

For a long time he lay there, his skin prickling from the heat of the shower, then he heaved himself up onto an elbow and picked up the receiver.

He pecked at the numbers with a finger. Away in the distance the bell rang and he wondered if the sun was shining or the rain beating on the roofs of the houses, jigging on the window panes so that you couldn't even see across the street let alone see the cormorants bobbing on the sea.

I will give it ten rings, he thought, then I will really have tried.

'Hello,' said his mother's voice in his ear. She sounded tired.

'Mum . . .' He paused, wondering what to say next. He saw her standing in the neat hall, the receiver clamped to her ear, as if she were afraid that his words might escape and never be recovered. He heard her quick breath. He heard her speak his name. 'Laurence?'

Unlike everyone else he knew, she always called him Laurence. 'Didn't I choose it against the world,' she had said to him once, 'because I liked it. It's as good a name as they come and there's no call for anyone to pass remarks about it.'

He had always suspected that she had named him for Laurence Olivier but had never had the courage to ask her if this was so.

'Laurence – are you all right? Where are you? You shouldn't do a thing like that. Davey!' She raised her voice and called down the hall towards his father's study. 'It's Laurence. It's Laurence!' She blew her nose. 'You are bad, Laurence. We . . .' She couldn't go on.

'Mum . . .'

He heard her mumble something and then his father's voice was in his ear.

'Where are you, Lar?'

'Dublin.'

'You should have let us know, son, before you went running off like that.'

Lar didn't answer. He was, he thought to himself, thirty-six – long past the age of having to answer for his actions.

'Lar?'

'I'm in Dublin. I'm all right. I just rang to let you know. It's raining cats and dogs.' He really didn't care if they were interested or not.

'Dublin's a good place, rain or shine,' said his father. 'When will you be back? Your mum would like to go down and clean up the place for you before—'

'No, thanks. I don't need her to do that. I'd rather she didn't do it. I don't know when I'll be back.'

'Term starts in a week.'

He didn't reply.

'Have you spoken to the Head?'

'I have spoken to no one. I don't know when I'll be back. I just rang to say that I was all right. I don't need to be interrogated.'

'Your mother has been upset.'

'No need.'

'Of course there's need.'

There was a long silence. Lar could hear his mother's voice. He wondered what she was wearing; grey, he supposed, she nearly always wore grey. He saw her quite clearly, wearing grey, standing by the grandfather clock, tears making her face ugly.

'I think we should talk, son. Would you like me to come down?' His father's voice was gentle.

'No. There is nothing to talk about.'

'Well, come home then. Come here and let us mind you until . . .'

'Until what?'

'Until you're well again.'

'There is nothing wrong with me.'

'You're not yourself.'

'I am myself. I am Laurence McGrane. I am a schoolteacher. I know who I am. I know my wife and child were murdered. I know I am acting in a wild and irrational way towards the people who say they love me. I know that one day I will return to normality and be quiet and polite and acceptable, but not yet. I want to be allowed to scream and burn and hate, until I am sickened by my self-indulgence. I haven't got a date for that. So fuck off Dad and stop trying to heal me.'

He had never sworn at his father before and the hand that held the receiver trembled as he did so.

There was a long pause.

'We do love you, son,' was all his father said, then he put down the phone and all Lar could hear was the emptiness of disconnection.

✳   ✳   ✳

Why does the telephone always ring when you are in the bath? One of life's mysteries.

I am not going to answer it. I am going to lie here in this sweet steam and let it ring.

I have to.

If I were to scramble out now and make a dash into my bedroom, I would undoubtedly open up my wound. So I will just lie here and wonder who it could be. What delicious alternatives to an evening at home in front of the telly watching Morse might be on offer? My sister wanting a babysitter? That just means watching Morse in front of her telly. My mother asking me over for a nourishing meal? She doesn't like Morse. Perhaps it's a friend. Poor Clara, she might be thinking (or he, if it comes to that), I haven't seen her for ages. Must give her a buzz and see if she's OK. See how she's recovering from her nasty op. Not worth opening up the wound for any of those calls.

Nah!

If, on the other hand, the call was from New York . . . Six-thirty minus five equals lunchtime in Manhattan; 'Forgive me, guys, I have a really important call to make. A life-and-death call.'

Deep breath.

Inhale steam.

Let it slowly out. Calm, calm.

Laugh – quietly, of course. No big hearty laugh.

The bell has stopped.

Not much persistence.

I will get out now, gently, and be prepared in case the caller tries again.

If it is my mother she surely will. She always tries twice. It pleases her to know that I don't wander far these days. Like a spancelled goat.

I love big soft towels; they are one of my extravagances. I buy them in the winter and the summer sales in posh shops – white, pale blue and pink, yellow and even a pepperminty green. I keep them neatly folded in soft layers in the cupboard by the hot press. I will leave them all to my sister Grace in my will; she and I have some similar tastes and she will appreciate the thought behind the bequest. But then, of course, I may see her out, in spite of my lifestyle.

What made me think of New York?

Silly question. How can I forget New York when every time I strip off and see my scarred belly, run my finger along the still tender flesh, I want to scream?

'Shithead bastard motherfucker fuckface gobshite.' My vocabulary is limited, but I feel better after that small explosion.

I will pour myself a good glass of Côtes Roties, right up to the brim and . . .

There it goes again.
Mother.
'Hello, Mother.'
'How did you know?'
'Second sight. I was in the bath.'
'Are you all right, dear?' Shade of anxiety in the voice.
'Fine. I went for a walk and got very wet. I just thought . . .'
'Sensible.'
'For once.'
She laughs.
'I just wondered if you'd like to pop round and have a bite to eat. I seem to have an awful lot of food.'
Bingo!
'Thanks awfully, but I'm afraid I can't.'
'What are you up to?'
'Oh, ah . . . nothing much. I just arranged to meet a friend for a drink.'
'Ah.' She doesn't believe me. Sensible woman. She's known me too long. 'Don't tire yourself out, dear.'
'No. I certainly won't do that.'
'Well . . .'
'Thanks, Mother.'
'That's all right. I'll see you in a day or so.'
'Yes. Bye.'
Perhaps that is what I will do. In my dry clothes I will walk up to the Druid's Chair, drink my glass of red wine there surrounded by living human beings and get back here in time for Morse. I really am beginning to feel restless. I must ask the doctor when I may leave again; even begin to make plans.

Sometimes plans are better than the reality.

Take New York, for instance: I certainly didn't plan *that* bloody debacle.

My planning was absolutely top hole; a year's lectureship at NYU and a flat, excuse me, apartment loaned to me by an acquaintance called Jodie who was taking a year's sabbatical travelling round India, in Morton Street, just a hop, skip and a jump from the university. Love never came into my plan at all. The odd delicious 'affaire', possibly; I had certainly not planned for love and its consequences.

Just get out. Open the door, snatch your brolly, get out of here and go up the road to the Druid's Chair rather than down that road of ridiculous remembering, that well-trodden road. A circular road that ends always where it began, never changes and always has the power to make me cry.

Out, woman!

How I love Irish rain. It gives us our soft skin and our luxuriant hair, or that's what they used to tell us anyway; I doubt if they say so any longer. I was so full of the belief of this that I used as a child to run out into the garden when it rained and turn my face up to the sky, allowing the drops to break on my skin and run in streams down my neck and shoulders. Someone always put a stop to this innocent pleasure quite quickly. It makes me laugh when I think of what fourteen-year-old kids get up to nowadays.

Sometimes famous people use this pub; the odd rock star, film-makers, actors, the occasional poet, a dramatist or two, not of course all at the same time. It is quite a discreet establishment, part of its charm being the possibility of reasonable conversation. This evening only a few locals have braved the rain and there is a corner seat where I can dump myself and sip the plonk and stare at nothing.

Perhaps I could now continue with *Shepherd on the Rock*? Wrong place. I need the open air, the wind for that.

'Clara! Did you walk up here in all that rain?'

'Umbrella, gum boots, macintosh. What are you doing here anyway? I thought doctors only drank in private.'

He puts his glass of Guinness down on the table beside my wine. 'Mind if I join you?'

'Not unless you're going to lecture me.'

He pulls out a chair and sits. He leans forward and picks up his drink.

'You get a good glass of Guinness here. After I finish my house calls I always allow myself a treat. Cheers.'

He takes a long drink.

He looks tired. He must be getting on. He has been our doctor for a long time. Twenty years anyway. I believe he is a keen fisherman. He doesn't smile much; I quite like that. I find doctors who smile a lot rather patronising. He pulls a packet of cigarettes out of his pocket and a lighter.

'I am being quite sinful. I do hope that you are my only patient here.' He lights up.

'So?' He speaks to me through a haze of smoke.

'So what?'

'What brings you up here in all that rain? You'd be better off tucked up in bed.'

'Or having supper with Mother.'

'Certainly.'

'I'm starting to feel stir crazy.'

'That's a good sign. It's the patients numbed by lethargy that you have to worry about.' He stared at me for a long time, his eyes slowly taking in every feature of my face. 'Don't do anything crazy for a while yet though. I'd like you under my eye for another few weeks.'

His eyes are a very dark brown. He must have some foreign blood somewhere inside him, Italian perhaps. It's a funny thing about brown eyes, they always look kinder than blue ones – maybe never so lively, but definitely kinder. Perhaps I should make a point of only falling in love with brown-eyed men.

But he is talking to me and I am not listening. I am following a foolish butterfly in my head.

'How old are you, Doctor?'

He stops talking and looks surprised. 'Probably old enough to be your father.'

'I doubt that.'

'Fifty on Thursday, if you really want to know.'

'A momentous age.'

'Or monumental.'

'Why did you never get married?'

'I could ask you the same question, but I won't be so foolish. Nobody seemed to want me enough to seek me out – I suppose that's the right answer. I have given it quite a bit of thought from time to time. I have a very good secretary and a very good housekeeper; my life is well ordered. I like order in my life.'

'Sex?'

'My dear Clara, you are obsessed with sex. Haven't I and several others just had to clean up the results of your obsession with sex?'

God, what a fool I am to have walked into this silly conversation. Now I am blushing and i can feel idiotic tears filling up my eyes. 'What a . . .'

He pulls a clean white handkerchief from his pocket and hands it to me. '. . . Rotten thing to say. Yes, I apologise. Blow your nose. Have another glass of wine.'

He touches my hand briefly.

'Forgive me.'

The tears begin to trickle down my cheeks.

'Doctor . . .'

Abruptly he picks up both our glasses and goes to the bar. I sniffle for a moment and blow my nose as ordered.

This is not like me: I must still be quite unwell, 'post-operative' as he said the other day. If I sit here snivelling and drinking glasses of red wine, I will miss Morse. Bear that in mind, my dear Clara.

He must have eyes in the back of his head because he doesn't return with the two glasses until I have composed myself. I give him his handkerchief.

'Thank you.'

He puts it back in his pocket.

He swallows and licks the froth from his lips and swallows again before either of us says a word.

'How are you going to celebrate your birthday?' I ask.

'My brother lives in Oughterard. I'm taking off for a few days, leaving my patients to their own devices, and I'm going down to stay with him. He is married, just in case you want to know. Lovely wife, four children. I think I will do some fishing. Mayfly time, you know.'

'That will be nice.'

'Yes. Four days of peace. No telephone, no anxious patients, no midnight panics, no hospital visiting, no meeting patients in pubs. They probably won't remember that it's my birthday so I won't even have to say thank you for a lot of presents. I can sit in a boat and when I'm not catching fish I can ponder on what I'm going to do with the next fifty years of my life.'

'Do you have a problem about that? You seem to me to be one of the few people I know who has a sense of purpose.'

'Do you find that boring? Tedious?'

'No. I admire it. It makes me feel a bit envious, like some silly adolescent, still looking for the right road. Unable to read the signposts.'

He sighs.

I wonder what he is thinking about – shining trout leaping in the sunlight as he reels them into his boat on Lough Corrib? Or should they be salmon? I don't know. I am quite ignorant when it comes to things like that.

Perhaps though he sighs because he is annoyed by the thought of me wandering round the world unable to read signposts. And all the other people like me.

Fifteen years older than I am and fifteen years, or thereabouts, younger than my mother. Piggy in the middle.

He glances at his watch.

'I have to go. My dinner will be ready. Drink that up quickly and I'll drive you home.'

'No, thanks. I can walk.'

'My dear Clara, don't be foolish. It is lashing. I insist on driving you home.'

'And I insist on staying here and drinking my wine in tiny little sips. Thank you all the same.'

He looks at me for a moment and I wonder if he's going to grab me and haul me out of the pub, but he just stands up and gives a little bow in my direction and walks off towards the door.

I feel quite foolish.

*　*　*

'Do you mind if I bring the dog in?'

'You have him brought?'

'Well, yes, but I . . .'

'As long as he doesn't torment, plague or defile the customers.'

'She won't do any of those things.'

'That's OK so.'

The barman rubbed at a stain on the bar with a greyish cloth. 'Mind you, if the place was full, that might be a different kettle of fish altogether.'

'I understand. A pint of Guinness, please.'

'There's some people doesn't like dogs.'

'That's true. I wouldn't want . . .'

'And there's some dogs doesn't like people.'

He placed a large glass under the tap and pulled the handle slowly down.

'From the North, are you?'

'Yes.'

'Thought I detected the blás. Down on a visit?'

'I . . .'

'Bet you need to get out of it once in a while. Get a breath of good fresh air.'

Lar thought of the good fresh North Sea air and smiled.

'Metamorphically speaking, of course.'

'Of course.'

'That'll be two pound and five pee. I suppose it costs less where you come from.'

'A bit,' said Lar.

'So I been told. There you go.' He pushed the glass towards Lar. 'Keep the hound under control.'

'Thanks.'

He picked up the glass and looked around for a seat. He felt Pansy's tail thumping against his leg. She was looking across the room to where a woman sat at a table on her own. Gently the dog pulled him towards her.

She looked up as they approached, startled for a moment by the sound of the dog's claws scrabbling on the floor. She didn't smile in any welcoming sort of way, but the dog drew him on until he stood beside her table. Pansy put her head on the woman's knee and smiled at her hopefully. Lar wondered if this constituted tormenting, plaguing or defiling.

'Sorry,' he said. 'She recognised you.'

The woman scratched the top of Pansy's head with a finger. 'Sorry, pal,' she said. 'No more biscuits. You're out of luck.' She looked up at Lar. 'Why don't you sit down? You're spilling your Guinness all over the floor. I'm going in a minute. I have to get home in time to see Morse.' She smiled briefly. 'I am addicted to Morse.'

'Isn't there someone sitting here?' He indicated the empty glass on the table.

She shook her head.

'He's gone. He leads a very orderly life. His dinner was waiting for him.'

'May I really?'

'Of course.'

Lar sat down and took a pull at his Guinness. Then he nudged Pansy under the table with his foot.

'How strange to meet you like this,' he said. 'How strange actually to walk into a pub here and meet anyone I know.'

She didn't say anything.

'Not, of course, that I know you. I could hardly say that.'

'Hardly.'

'But you know what I mean?'

She nodded.

He took another pull at the Guinness and glanced at her. Still pale, she looked as if she might have been crying. Her fingers fidgeted on the table by her glass. Thin and pale too, they were. Altogether she looked as if she'd been in the dark for a long time. He thought suddenly about Caitlin, heard for a moment her voice in his ear.

'*Lar.*'

He shook his head to dislodge the sound.

'I presume you live near here.'

She nodded again.

'Nice part of the world. We're in that hotel down by the harbour.'

'We?'

'Pansy and I.'

'On holiday?'

'I don't know.'

'What an odd thing to say.'

'I just came on an impulse. I had . . . stayed here before. I knew it. I'm doing a bit of thinking. This is a good place to think.'

She laughed.

'For some, perhaps. I have my mother down the road. She discourages thinking. She thinks it's bad for your blood pressure.'

'The lady who makes the biscuits?'

'The very one. You're from the North.'

'Glens of Antrim.'

'I hear it's very beautiful up there.'

'Yes. You should go and have a look some day. See for yourself.'

She shook her head.

'It's not on my itinerary. I've never been further north than Drogheda. Even there you can smell the disease when the wind is in the wrong direction.'

He put his glass on the table and stared at her. 'Would that be the attitude of many people down here?'

'Quite a number. Just ask around and you'll see for yourself.'

'Disease?'

'Terminal hatred – infectious, contagious, hereditary. A bit like AIDS – incurable.'

'You're a bigot?'

'I suppose I must be. We're all bigots when push comes to shove. Personally I think I'm just tired and a bit cynical, and of course I didn't mean to imply that you are diseased, merely at risk.' She checked her watch, a large gold man's watch that looked, he thought, as if it had cost one hell of a lot of money. 'I have to go.'

She drained the dregs from her glass and stood up, frowning

slightly. Under the table Pansy thumped her tail. 'Why don't you come home and watch Morse with me?'

He was confused by her invitation. So apparently was she. Her pale face had become red.

'Sorry,' she said. 'I didn't mean to . . . well, you know. After all, I owe you one. You saved me from the possibility of suicide. Maybe you don't like Morse.'

She turned to go. Pansy scrambled out from under the table and looked at her, smiling.

Lar pushed his half-full glass to one side.

'Thanks,' he said, getting up. 'That'd be great. I'd like that.'

He followed her across the bar. At the door he turned and raised his hand towards the barman, who in turn raised his eyebrows. Oh God, thought Lar, what am I getting into?

It was still raining. She put up her umbrella and started off back down the road towards Dalkey without a word. She walked quite slowly and from time to time dragged her right leg for a moment as if she were in pain. He wondered whether to offer her his arm, but decided against it. This was an unpredictable sort of a woman.

They turned down a sloping laneway overhung with the leaning branches, not yet quite in leaf, of tall trees. She pushed open a resisting gate and they walked along a short brick path to a small cottage.

Well, she's not a gardener, he thought, looking at the tangles of weeds and shrubs in the bed along the front wall of the house.

'I'm not a gardener.' She spoke the words as she pushed the key into the front door. He blushed.

The house was warm. He hung his wet coat on a hook in the hall and followed her into some sort of sitting room, Pansy padding close by him, as if glued to his leg.

She began to fiddle with the television remote control. 'Sometimes this doesn't work,' she said. 'I think it may need a new battery or something. Do those yokes need batteries?'

He took it from her.

'I'll do it.'

'Of course,' she murmured and left the room.

The damn thing didn't seem to work.

Pansy, happy to be in someone's home, stretched out on a mat in front of the unused fireplace and thumped her tail contentedly a couple of times and then appeared to go to sleep.

Lar found the television set. There seemed to be no sign of life, no little red or green lights, no flashing symbols of any sort. He followed the flex behind a pile of books and a sofa until he found a plug set in the skirting. It was switched off.

'Bingo,' he said aloud and switched it on. It was simple. A little red light came on in the set, he pressed a button on the remote and the screen flashed into life. A man with a very red face was talking Irish. He pressed another button and a large packet of washing powder thrust its bulk onto the screen.

The woman came into the room with some cheese and bread on a tray and a bottle of wine.

'Aren't you clever.'

'It wasn't switched on.'

She put the tray on a table and laughed.

'Well, there you go. I am a technological idiot. Would you

ever open the wine and I'll make you a cheese sandwich. Perhaps you're not hungry?'

'A cheese sandwich would be great.'

She buttered bread.

'I'm going to sit on the sofa with my feet up. My doctor thinks I ought to be in bed and that's the next best thing. "Rest," he keeps saying to me. "Rest, rest." I could strangle him. I get so bored resting and I get so tired doing things. Of course none of that is his fault. Pour it out, there's a good chap.'

'What's the matter with you? If you don't mind my asking.'

'No. I don't.' She put a couple of chunks of cheese onto the bread and then pushed it across the table towards him. She flopped down onto the sofa and lay back among the cushions for a moment, closing her eyes and looking, he thought, shocking awful.

'I've had all my insides out. All the important bits, I mean. I am no longer to all intents and purposes a woman. Just a thing walking round the world. A useless empty bag of some sort.'

'You look like a woman to me.'

She opened her eyes and looked at him.

'A bit tired,' he said, 'but definitely a woman. Who but a woman would try and get pictures from a TV without turning on the power first?'

He handed her a glass of wine.

'Thanks. My name is Clara, by the way. I wasn't going to tell you, but then I thought, Why the hell not?'

She reached out and took a piece of cheese which she began to chew carefully. 'Are you sure we're on the right channel? I don't want to miss a second.'

'Laurence McGrane.'
'Laurence McGrane.' She mimicked his North Antrim accent.
'And we *are* on the right channel.'

* * *

> De spring is sprung, de grass is ris.
> I wonder where de flowers is?
> De boid is on de wing,
> But dat's absoid,
> How can de boid be on de wing?
> De wing is on de boid.

Why do such silly things wake me?

Why is that silly piece of doggerel leaping in my head? Why not the more salubrious *Der Frühling will kommen, der Frühling meine Freud'*?

The sun is trying to push its way through the clouds. I can see that with my eyes half open.

My mother will ring me soon. 'I hope I didn't wake you, darling?'

'Of course not,' I will say. 'I have been up for ages.'

She will know that to be untrue, but she will make no comment.

Morse was mediocre. That happens sometimes; too full of slightly pointless convolutions. Not that that bothered the man, Laurence, Larry or Lar. He fell asleep quite fast, round about the middle of the first episode. He never stirred during the first commercial break when I went to get myself a glass of water. He looked as he leaned back into the chair like a man who hadn't had a good sleep in front of a television set for a long time. I felt quite disturbed for him.

I must say, he and the dog went quietly when I woke them both as the credits rolled and sent them on their way, out into the rain. I did feel enough anxiety on their behalf to shove my umbrella into his hand at the door.

'Take it. Take it.' I remember saying that. I don't remember what he said, but he took it and put it up and they splashed down the path to the gate. I do hope he found his way back to that dismal hotel. Awful to be found drowned in a pothole halfway down Killiney Hill Road.

I must unroll myself and crawl out of bed. Each day I try to do it earlier than the day before and with more dexterity. That thought makes me open my eyes a fraction more and look at my watch – my rich gold watch. I saw that Laurence person eyeing it. One day when i am really better I will throw it away. Drop it in the sea perhaps or better still, place it face up on the railway line and stand and watch while the Dart or the Wexford Express scrunches it into a thousand small expensive pieces. It's the only watch I've ever had, since I was a child that is. Then I seem to remember a Mickey Mouse watch, those long accusatory fingers saying, 'Late again, Clara,' so often that I stopped wearing one as I grew up, preferring to be late without guilt.

'You'll be late for your own funeral.' I can hear James's slightly high-pitched drawl, amused, a touch angry too, and, I thought, loving, as he took the watch from his wrist and clasped it round mine. It was heavy and warm and I thought I would wear it for a few days and then return it to him, warm also from my body and he would love that warmth.

Nothing ever happens the way we plan.

I must get up. I must not dwell on such debilitating thoughts. I suppose being old will be like this; the awful care with which you have to make those first movements after waking; wondering when will the pain start and will it be grand agony or just the small niggling kind; which elbow can I lean on today without causing the cramps in my belly to activate themselves? All something to look forward to, I dare say. This must be a rehearsal for the future.

As I punch my pillows into some sort of supportive shape i wonder what James said to his wife about his watch. It is the sort of watch that you can't help noticing and also therefore, you can't help noticing the absence of it on a person's wrist. The heavy plaited gold strap embraced his bony wrist as if it were made for it. I wonder what lie he told her when she asked about its absence. I'm sure, whatever it was, it came trippingly off his tongue. Maybe, of course, he just went out and bought himself another one, so she will never have noticed. He had more money than sense, that was for sure, and more charming deceit than any other man I have ever known.

I should feel sorry for her, James's wife, but of course I don't; her presence has destroyed my life. She doesn't have to say anything or move or even be aware of my presence . . . this is, of course, all quite untrue, early-morning blues. Even if she hadn't existed, i would still be the ill, barren woman that he made me. His gift to me was not a million-dollar watch, it was the emptiness of my future.

Telephone.

She's early today. Get the feet on the floor, so that I do not have to tell a lie. 'Hello.'

'I hope I didn't wake you, darling.'

'Of course not. I have been up for hours.'

'What are your plans for the day?'

Slight pause. I can hear her soft waiting breaths. 'Well . . .'

'I thought you might like to go for a short drive. Powerscourt, Greystones, the Sally Gap. A little walk. Some fresh air and—'

'No,' I interrupt her. 'Thanks, but no. I can't.'

Another pause.

'Thanks all the same. I have plans. All-day plans.' I could feel her disbelief down the line. 'I have to catch up with a lot of things – letters, pay some bills. And I've arranged to meet someone on Killiney Hill for a walk. A nice man, you'd like him. He has a dog. I've arranged . . . I can't . . . So you see.'

She sighed.

'I've decided to write a novel.'

First time I've spoken these words aloud.

'Darling, what a good idea. You've had so many strange experiences. I've always thought . . .'

'So I need to get organised before I start on that. You know, clear up the mess.'

'Perhaps you might come and have supper?'

'Yes. Thank you, I'd like that.'

'I'll come and collect you about seven.'

'Mother, I can walk.'

'I don't want you overdoing things.'

'Five minutes' walk. I'll see you just after seven. Have to fly. The kettle is boiling.'

End of conversation.

I will not get back into bed. I will go and put the kettle on and think about the novel I am now committed to write.

✳   ✳   ✳

Caitlin held him and rocked him gently in her arms, his head crooked on her shoulder, as he had seen her hold the child so often.

'If I were the painter,' he had said, 'I could paint you both now. Madonna and Child with rocks and sea.'

She laughed. 'What a sentimentalist you are.'

'Halo, blue dress, crinkling hair . . .'

'Wrong-sex baby.'

'Who's to know?'

With a swift movement she handed him the child, who laughed and reached to touch his face.

'On the other hand,' she said, jumping to her feet, 'I am the painter. Perhaps I should paint you. Father and Child. A modern sacred icon.' She scrabbled for paper and pencil.

'Halo,' she murmured. 'Blue shirt, crinkling hair, right-sex baby.'

The sound of the sea had been in his ears as he sat with the child circled in his arms. Her warm breath was on his neck and the only sounds were the waves shifting below them and the tiny scratch of Caitlin's pencil.

'What,' she asked after a long silence, 'do you think would be the male equivalent of Madonna and Child?'

He shifted in bed and the pillows were no longer the comforting arms, the bed was in fact quite comfortless. He could still hear the sound of the sea though, like the breath of the child in his ears. A living child.

He opened his eyes and saw the thread of blue, the promise of sun pushing its way through the crack between brown velvet curtains. If it weren't for Pansy, he thought, I could lie here all day staring at the ceiling. I could hang that bit of cardboard on the door knob, *Do Not Disturb*, and they would presume that I was fucking some young one picked up last night in that pub at the top of the hill.

He grinned when he thought of the one who had picked him up, then he remembered the umbrella and swung his legs out of the bed and stretched his bare arms out towards the crack of light that hit the ceiling just above his head.

He took Pansy for a short run down to the harbour before breakfast and she twirled her tail with happiness and barked at a couple of bored seagulls that sat on the low stone wall. Two men were putting lobster pots into a small boat which bucked under them, impatient to be released from the ropes that held it to the shore. The smells were of seaweed and salt and decaying fish.

If only.

Dead dreams.

If only I had gone with them, I wouldn't be here now to say *if only*.

Mother and Father would have taken Pansy. Father would have liked a companion for his daily walks.

That would all be so much more orderly.

Then he thought of his mother standing by the clock, dressed in grey.

'Wouldjever throw us over that rope there?' one of the men called to him from the bronco boat.

Lar nodded and pulled the loop of rope from a metal bollard and threw it across the couple of feet of water between the shore and the boat.

'Champion,' said the fisherman. Released, the boat clattered away.

'Good luck,' Lar called after them, but they weren't listening. 'So,' he said to Pansy, who wasn't listening either, 'we'll go and have breakfast and then we'll bring that Clara back her umbrella. If we can remember where she lives.'

He couldn't.

The roads looked so different in the daylight and he wandered for a long time past hedges and gates, peering into alleyways, but nothing resembling her cottage could he find. Maybe it didn't exist. Maybe she didn't exist, maybe he had never slept through practically a whole episode of Morse.

Still clutching the umbrella, he found the gate to the park and went in and up the hill. Uneasy grey clouds were blowing quite fast across the sky. She was there, standing on the edge again, listening, he presumed, to the music in her head.

He stood for a while and watched her, then gently called her name. 'Clara.'

She turned at once, almost as if she had been waiting, and smiled at him. 'Good morning. I hope you slept well?'

'I'm sorry about that.'

'That's OK. At least you didn't snore.'

'I've brought this.' He shook the umbrella at her. 'I tried to find your house, but I couldn't. I'm not endowed with a good sense of direction. I always need a navigator.'

'Thank you.' She took the umbrella from him and looked at

it with distaste. 'I hate umbrellas. I'm sure it's something to do with *Mary Poppins*. My mother used to read *Mary Poppins* to us ad nauseam.'

'You're rather hard on your mother, aren't you?'

She turned away and looked out to sea again.

'I don't want to be like her, that's all – and I probably will. The temptation to be nice is pretty overpowering. Anyway, it's none of your business.'

He wondered if that was a dismissal. He took a couple of steps away from her, backwards, awkward steps. Pansy, taken by surprise, yelped as he stood on her paw.

'Oh God, Pansy. I am so sorry.' He bent down to comfort her; when he straightened up again Clara was standing with a biscuit in her outstretched hand. Disloyal Pansy was there in a flash pulling the biscuit gently from the woman's fingers.

'She's saving me from myself,' said Clara apologetically. 'Otherwise I would eat them all. I don't really want to become like a barrage balloon, but it will happen if I don't find enough people to share my mother's biscuits with. It's a plot of hers. She longs to see me roly-poly comfortable and with my feet anchored to the ground.'

'It's going to take a lot of biscuits,' he said. A single raindrop exploded on his cheekbone. 'Damn.'

He looked up at the sky. There was no grey cloud directly above him. He wiped at the wetness with a finger.

'Rain,' he said.

She nodded. She pushed a biscuit into her mouth and chewed at it vigorously. 'Rain,' she agreed through a mouthful of crumbs.

Another drop hit him between the eyes. I am a target, he thought. Here I stand under this circle of blue and . . . another one.

Two, three, four.

She was saying something to him.

She was pointing at the umbrella in his hand.

He nodded and fumbled and the umbrella opened and he held it up between himself and the rapidly diminishing circle of blue and she moved towards him and took his arm. She was still talking and the rain was tapping on the nylon arch over their heads.

'Coffee.'

He heard the word.

She pulled at his arm. 'You're not listening.'

'I'm sorry.'

'You owe me a cup of coffee.'

'Yes. I . . . of course. Of course.'

She was pulling him along, back over the brow of the hill, past the obelisk, along the path now freckled with raindrops. Pansy galumphed beside them.

'I was thinking about Schubert.'

He was hearing her now.

'You know the way you get something stuck in your head? The same old tune, on and on, sometimes for days and days. Well, at this moment it's "Shepherd on the Rock". An echoing song. It's very appropriate. I stand on that cliff and sing, and in my head the echo comes back from the hills, Little Sugarloaf and all that. All those hills, over there.' She jerked her thumb back over her shoulder. 'You may not have noticed them,' she went on. 'You don't really look around you much, do you? I love Schubert. I feel so connected into Lieder, or three or four instruments working in together. I prefer that to huge symphonic works. Grand operas make me want to go and bury myself in a hole. You know, I don't think they'll let Pansy into a caff. People have got very strange about things like dogs and so on. We'd better go back to my house. Or your hotel. I suppose we could go there? What do you think?'

He opened his mouth to say he didn't really care, but no sound came out.

'I expect my coffee will be better than theirs and you won't have to put poor old Pansy in the car.'

Her steps faltered for a moment and she leant briefly on his arm. 'He died young, you know. Thirty-two. At least, I consider that to be young. Just think of all that achievement. I bet you're more than thirty-two. I am anyway. And what have you done? Excuse me, maybe you've done a lot of achieving. I haven't. I've done a lot of travelling and taught quite a number of people about Elizabeth Bowen and Kate O'Brien. A lot of travelling, but no achieving. I keep thinking about Schubert, Keats, Mozart, J.C. Look what they achieved. They all died young.'

'J.C.?' he asked and then realised his foolishness. 'Oh, yes. J.C.'

'In terms of achievement, not of course Godishness. I'm not talking about that sort of thing.'

'I'm not really sure what you're talking about.' His voice was peevish. He liked people to make sense; he always had. Even Caitlin had annoyed him from time to time by talking what he felt to be whimsical nonsense, or perhaps as she had sometimes suggested, he hadn't been listening to her in the right way. Perhaps his ears had sometimes been too full of common sense. His mother and father had been keen on common sense. I must ring them up again. I must. I must.

Clara was blathering on by his side, her face wet with rain turned up towards him. He had let the umbrella slip to one side and while he was dry, the rain toppled onto her face and shoulders.

'. . . And of course there was Chatterton, the marvellous boy – he was even younger. A child. *Oh, synge unto me roundelaie, O droppe the brynie tears with me . . .'*

He adjusted the umbrella; she didn't appear to notice.

'Batty, of course, but at least he did do something. How awful, how truly awful to think that you might die without doing anything, leaving anything memorable.' She pulled at his sleeve with her fingers.

'Yes,' he answered.

'That is why I wasn't contemplating the terminal jump the other day.'

'I didn't really think you were.'

'You gave the impression . . .'

'You took the impression . . .'

She nodded. 'Maybe. Yes. That's the sort of thing I do.'

The rain slid from the branches above their heads, bounded from the ground below them, came at them from every direction. The umbrella, he thought, was an irrelevance. If he had been alone he would have run, splashing through the puddles, but he could see that she was moving her fastest and relying more and more on the support of his arm.

As they stood by the edge of the road waiting for a safe moment to cross, the passing cars threw greasy water in their direction. There was no longer blue to be seen anywhere and the clouds seemed to press lower and lower, now almost tangling with the branches of the trees.

She sighed. 'God, how I long to be away,' she said aloud but to no one in particular.

'I've never been out of the British Isles,' he said. They stepped across the water running by the pavement and made their way over the road. Several cars had switched on their sidelights and the reflections flickered on the wet road.

'Caitlin,' he said, and then stopped. Clara looked at him. His lips were firmly buttoned. She hustled him down the laneway that he had been unable to find earlier.

All three of them shook themselves once they were in her tiny hall, dog, man and woman. Clara laughed and then took their coats and hung them on hooks behind the door.

'How silly we look, shaking ourselves like that – not Pansy, of course.'

Pansy wagged her tail on hearing her name.

'Who is Caitlin? Come into the kitchen. I'll put the kettle on.'

He wanted to say no one, which was of course true, but thought how unfair that would be and anyway, this woman wouldn't let him get away with that. She had an Aga. Caitlin had always wanted an Aga. She pushed the large kettle onto the hotplate, then bent down and rubbed at Pansy with a drying-up cloth.

'Mud,' she muttered. She stood up, red in the face from stooping and looked at him. 'Sit down, man. For heaven's sake sit down and tell me who Caitlin is.'

54

'She's dead.'

He pulled a chair out from the table and sat down. She threw the muddy cloth across the room.

'Oh. I'm sorry. I—'

'She always wanted to travel. Circumnavigate the world. We would have one day.' He laughed harshly. 'That's what I always said. "One day. One day. Next year. Leave it a while, love, till we're on our feet." This is as far as I've got. Dublin's fair city.'

'Tea or coffee?'

'Coffee.' After a long pause he said, 'Please.'

Pansy had arranged herself stretched out in front of the Aga; her ribs rose and fell, her face relaxed into a smile.

'She was my wife.'

Three large spoons of coffee into the pot. She pulled the steaming kettle across the plate and tilted it forward; a silver arc of water hissed onto the coffee. She didn't look in his direction. She put the jug of coffee onto the table and balanced the plunger on top.

'Looking back on it now, when it's too late, I can see how silly I was. We were on our feet. I'm a teacher – Maths. Head of the department. No problems. We could have taken off during those long summers and gone wherever she wanted to go, but I bloody well always said no. I was so happy at home, I just couldn't conceive how I could be any happier anywhere else. And I thought that for her too. Put my thoughts into her head. She never complained – well, not like I've heard other women complain. She just gave a little shrug with her shoulders.'

Clara fetched two mugs from the dresser and the milk from

the fridge and he never said another word as she moved around the room. He just watched her domestic movements with a certain pleasure. Finally she sat down at the table and pushed the plunger in the coffee-pot.

'What happened her?' She asked the question apprehensively, not knowing whether he wanted her to ask it or not.

He rubbed at the side of his nose for a moment with a finger. 'She was killed in a motor accident.'

'I'm sorry.'

'And the child, Moya. She was named for my mother. Caitlin wasn't sure whether she liked the name or not.'

'How dreadful.' She touched his shoulder gently. 'I'm really sorry. I shouldn't have.'

'. . . Eleven months and three days. A short life but a merry one.'

Clara was startled by the viciousness in his voice. 'I, ah . . .'

She poured a cup of coffee and pushed it across the table towards him. 'I . . .'

'You don't have to say anything. Too many people have said it all. Too many fucking words. I prefer silence.'

She nodded and sat down.

There was silence for a long time.

The dog seemed content enough, grunting from time to time in her sleep.

Finally Lar spoke.

'She was a lovely girl – woman. She hated being called a girl.'

Clara poured milk into her coffee.

'Caitlin.' He spoke the name as if it were some magic word.

'Yes. A nice name. Would you like some brown bread and jam?'

He shook his head.

'Or a biscuit, perhaps?'

'I'm OK.'

'Prozac?'

'Just coffee. Coffee's fine.'

They lapsed into silence once more and Clara asked herself if it would be rude to get down to the *Irish Times* crossword. Yes, it would, she decided, so she just sat there and listened to the murmur of the kettle on the Aga and wondered if she felt better than she had yesterday and thought that she probably did. I must tell Doctor, she thought, and then remembered that he would be in Oughterard by now. What dark thoughts was the man beside her thinking? She cast around for something to say to someone who preferred silence. However, he spoke first.

'Are you married?' He didn't sound very interested.

'No. Just post-operative.'

He didn't think that was particularly funny.

'We were so happy,' he told her. 'I never realised that such happiness was possible. It is something quite extraordinary, you know.'

'Yes, I'm sure it is.'

'I never thought anything like that could happen. I used to pooh pooh at fairytales and then I found I was living in this bubble of . . . I don't know how to explain without sounding silly. Insulated, that's what we were – insulated. Yes. Am I boring you?'

She shook her head.

'Your coffee will get cold.'

He picked up his mug and held it, both hands circling it. 'You say you keep travelling. Before I met her, I used to have such dreams of travelling, getting everything out of my system, forgetting . . .'

'Forgetting what?'

'Ireland. All that stuff we've been living through. Hateful stuff. Yes, hateful! Perhaps, I thought once, I will never come back. I will become another person in some other country and when anyone asks me where I come from, I will be able to say another name. Not Northern Ireland – Ulster – call it what you will. I would be able to pretend that that place had nothing to do with me. I could feel clean. I really wanted to feel clean.' He ducked his head and took a sip of coffee.

He's definitely a bit crazy, thought Clara.

'But.'

The word hung in the air between them. He took another drink. He looked at her, wondering what he should tell her.

Why should I tell her anything?

I could just go now; collect the dog and go.

I could leave my half-drunk coffee on the table. Walk out. Yeah.

'Why clean?' she asked then.

'I haven't ever felt clean. I grew up feeling – oh, I don't know, if not dirty, certainly polluted.'

She scratched at the end of her nose with a finger and sighed.

'So?' she said.

'What do you mean, so?'

'I mean, you've started a story, so get on with it. You were there, somewhere up there, feeling dirty and then you said "But." But?'

'I met Caitlin.'

'Dancing?'

She held out her hands towards him and smiled. The lights twirled, flashed, burst in cornucopias of colour.

'I don't dance.'

'Don't be silly. Everyone can dance.' She took his hand and pulled him into the music. 'You just wiggle your feet. Wiggle your body. Listen to the beat. Any fool can dance. You don't have to dance well, but at least try.'

'Well?'

'Well, things were different after that.'

'Love at first sight.'

He laughed.

'I suppose so. Is that foolish?'

'It's as good a way as any.'

'She had just left art college. I had led a very sheltered life – very boring, you might call it. I had never met anyone like her, with her energy, her love for being alive. And for some reason that I will never be able to work out, she liked me too.'

'I expect you're a very nice man.'

'Is that enough?'

'It's pretty good for starters.'

'So we got married.'

'Just like that.' She clicked her fingers.

He nodded. 'Everyone thought we were mad. "Wait a bit," they said. "Where's the rush? You have all your lives ahead of you. Get to know each other. This is a mighty step you're taking.

Think about it a while." We paid not a blind bit of attention to them and just went ahead. Well, I have to admit that I would have taken things a bit slower – gone in for the church and all that – but she wasn't having any of it.

' "What's wrong with the register office?" she said. "Why spend all that money and energy on all the other carry-on? We only do that for our parents. I don't want to get married for my parents. It's just you and me. That's what I want." Oh God, I remember I had a few bad nights over that. I thought my mother would go mad. Caitlin just laughed. "Sure she'll come round in time," she said. "And it won't bother God too much. He's got more important things on His mind, or at any rate He bloody well ought to have." She was like that. Impulsive. Very modern, I suppose. Wonderful.'

'Go on. Go on.' Clara wiggled her backside into a more comfortable position on her chair. 'I love listening to stories.' She looked at his face and then put out a hand and touched him. 'Sorry. That sounds really crass. Maybe that's what I am, a crass voyeur of some sort. I love sitting and trying to work out the truth from the fiction. Most people tell you quite a lot of lies when they begin to talk about themselves.'

He felt his face go red.

'I don't . . .'

'I don't mean lies, I mean embroidery of the truth – *structuring* the truth. The truth is never structured in reality. It's all over the place; sometimes untellable. So, you got married?'

He nodded.

'And your family? Were they . . .?'

'My mother was upset, yes. I hated that. I didn't want to

hurt anyone. My father said nothing, absolutely nothing, but she . . . well, I think she thought I was laying myself open to some dreadful retribution. She believes in the dreadfulness of God as well as in His loving kindness.' He smiled sadly. 'She's old-fashioned. Anyway, we got married, just as Caitlin wanted us to. No fuss. No carry-on. A few pals, a few jars. A very expensive meal, just the two of us. Roscoffs. Have you heard of Roscoffs?'

'Yes. Everyone's heard of Roscoffs. Belfast's best.'

'She didn't want to go there, but I persuaded her. I felt gross extravagance was important at that moment. The bride wore black. I didn't tell my mother that.' He took a drink of coffee and swished the liquid round and round in his mouth for a few moments before swallowing it.

'My mother's really very nice,' he said at last.

'I'm sure she is.'

'And she liked Caitlin a lot. A lot. She just has this . . .'

The telephone rang.

'. . . thing about religion.'

He paused.

She didn't move.

'Aren't you going to answer it?'

'No. I'm busy. Can't you see I'm busy? I'm listening.'

'It might be something important.'

She shook her head.

'No one who matters.'

'How do you know?'

'I know.'

'It could be a surprise.'

'I don't like surprises. It's probably my mother. She rings a lot. She worries about me.'

The telephone stopped ringing. She spread her hands wide. 'See?'

'I can never leave a telephone to ring. I can unplug it, I've done that occasionally, but once it starts to ring I have to pick it up.'

A flicker of a smile crossed her face.

'I have been addicted in my day, but I've cured myself.' Without being aware of what she was doing, she caught hold of the fine watch on her wrist and turned it round and round over her thin bones. 'Go on.'

'On?'

'Caitlin, your mother. You were telling me.'

'Yes. My mother liked her well enough, once she got to know her. She just didn't like our situation. She never considered that we were really married. She used to drop little hints . . . rock-like hints, really, and we would pretend that we didn't catch on. It became a bit tedious, but there wasn't anything that we could do. We didn't like to hurt her feelings any more than we already had. She calmed down in the end. I think she prayed a lot for us. She believes very much in the power of prayer. Supplication. Is your mother a religious lady?'

Clara thought about that.

'I don't know. That sounds a bit daft. When we were kids, when my father was alive, we . . . well, we observed the rituals. He had to really, it was bred into his bones. His father was a bishop.'

'A bishop?'

'Ever heard of Protestants?'

'Sorry.'

'My mother sort of eased off with the churchgoing after he died and now I don't think she ever goes at all, except for weddings and funerals. She might be a believer in her head, though. We never talk about it. She makes jam.'

'What's that supposed to mean?'

'I don't know. I just said it.'

'It's nothing to do with God.'

'I'm not so sure. It's a sign of her generosity. She gives us jam and cakes and biscuits and such a lot of love, and it doesn't matter what we do or say or where we go, she's always ready with the jam. She is somewhere safe to hide. Isn't that really what God is all about?'

'You never learnt much theology.'

'That's true enough. Have some more coffee?'

'No, thanks.' He pushed his cup away across the table and started to laugh.

'What's funny?' she asked.

'Somewhere safe to hide. That's what's funny. Your grandfather was a bishop and you have these weird notions.'

'He died before I was born. I believe he was a very benign fellow, a classical scholar. My mother liked him. He had a fine baritone voice — she admired that. I can't sing a note, though I like to pretend I can. I think I may get my desire to be able to sing from him, but lack his talent. Pity really.'

She poured herself some more coffee.

'I am stupidly addicted to this poison. Go on, tell me more

about Caitlin. Where did you live? Just give a few basic bits of information.'

He got up and walked over to the window; tiny leaf buds on a clematis crowded against the glass.

'You should cut your creeper back,' he said. 'Soon you won't be able to see out.'

'Thanks.'

'You're welcome.'

'I am a total stranger. You can tell me everything or nothing, lies or truth. It doesn't matter. It's of no consequence what you say to me.'

'Man and boy.'

'Sorry?'

He turned round to face her.

Der Frühling will kommen . . . the words floated softly into her head.

'In the same wee town, man and boy. Just looking out over the ocean. Perhaps that's why I like Killiney Hill.'

Der Frühling meine Freud'.

'But we had nothing out beyond us, maybe a Scottish island or two and then nothing. That is a wonderful feeling.'

She nodded. *Nun mach'ich mich fertig.*

'My father was a bank manager. One long main street. Maybe you don't know the North. We specialise up there in these long main streets.'

She'd seen them on television – rubble and drifting smoke, gaping windows, people made dispirited by the knowledge of their own uncompromising hatred.

'We live at one end of the street and the bank is at the other

64

end. Each day he would do that walk, up and back; he still does, just out of habit, morning and afternoon. "Yes, Davey," people say when they pass him. "How are you doing?" They do the same to me. "Yes, Lar." That's the way we greet each other. Maybe you don't know that.'

She shook her head.

'Nobody even says hello to you down here. Nobody catches your eye.'

'Perhaps you haven't been here long enough for people to get used to your face. Perhaps you don't smile enough.'

He looked a bit disconcerted.

'Excuse me using the word, but you do look — well, glum.'

He laughed. He threw his head back and laughed richly.

She watched him and drank some more coffee. He continued to laugh — a bit overdone, she thought, on the back of such a mild comment. He fumbled in his pocket and brought out a Kleenex; he wiped his eyes and then abruptly the laughter stopped.

'Why did I do that?' he asked her. 'What you said about me wasn't particularly funny.'

'I suppose you just needed to laugh. Any excuse for a laugh, as they say.'

'Hysteria?'

'Something like that.'

He sat down and rubbed at his face with his hand.

'I don't really sleep very well. I have dreams that I don't want to have. I keep struggling to wake up and I can't. It's as if someone is holding my eyes closed and then dragging these scenes across the inside of my eyelids. Terrible scenes of . . .' He stopped. He put his hand up to his mouth to stop the words falling out.

There was a long silence. Clara could hear the rain flooding the gutters and the distant sound of cars on the main road.

'Look,' she said eventually, 'I think you should go back to your hotel, pack up and check out. You can come and stay here for a few days. Both of you. You wouldn't have to keep Pansy in the car then. Just a few days, mind you. I have a little spare room upstairs.' She pointed towards the ceiling. 'Perhaps you might sleep better there. Hotels are so, I don't know. Horribly empty.'

He didn't say anything. She leant forward and nudged his knee with a hand.

'Yes, Lar,' she said. 'How are you doing?'

He smiled.

'It's very kind of you, but . . .'

'But me no buts. I'm not coming on at you, I promise you that.'

His face went pink. He shook his head.

'Nor, of course, do I want to force you to do something that you don't want to do. Why don't you go away and think about it? Consult Pansy. I bet she'd prefer it here. Then, either come back with your things or don't. As you see fit. OK?'

He got up.

He snapped his fingers and Pansy moved unwillingly from her place by the Aga. Her claws clicked on the tiled floor as she walked over to him. She stood looking up into his face, her tongue lolling from the side of her mouth.

'It's a very kind suggestion. Very. We'll give it serious consideration, won't we, girl?'

He snapped his fingers again and left the kitchen, Pansy clicking by his side.

'Take the umbrella,' Clara called after them.

✳ ✳ ✳

Der Frühling will kommen,
der Frühling meine Freud';
nun mach'ich mich fertig,
zum Wandern bereit.

Itchy feet.

Perhaps, perhaps I can anchor myself here.

Who was it said 'apply the seat of the pants to the seat of the chair' — something like that? Will I be able to persuade the itch in the feet to become the itch in the fingers? Let them do the wandering. For a while anyway, just until I can stand up straight, run if need be, laugh. For God's sake, I have to be able to laugh before I go wandering again!

Switch on.

cccllmmm.

Your friendly Mac is now at your service.

Your service. Fonts, files, disks, folders, mouse, all at your disposal, waiting for the clicks and double clicks. Smiling at you. Please smile back. Please click.

Put the first mark on that endless page, a page that isn't a page but a door, opening into mysterious space. Place your mark with caution, because this may be a road of pain that you don't want to travel along.

Or don't start at all, if you're afraid. Shut down.

I know how to create sentences, construct phrases, make sense out of obscurity. I have earned my living for years doing just that, but that's not the point. Will i be able to discard all that academic carving and exploring and teach myself to breathe life and energy into those little black insects that are what I will have to work with? I have little choice. I must now try to create my children on the endless page, or live barren.

I will not be barren.

Roll up your sleeves Clara. Click. Double click. Switch on.

cccclllmmm.

Tomorrow perhaps.

No.

Today.

The rain guards me like prison bars from the world. Move. Get the fingers cracking before that guy, that Laurence comes back with his wet dog and his suitcase; before I have to go and have dinner with Mother. Oh God, i'll have to bring him too and she will get ideas, mighty notions in her head. I can feel her mapping out my future, making plans. She does, of course, have an inherent dislike of people from the North of Ireland – a mistrust I should say, rather than dislike – so she will regard him with suspicion and wonder how to protect me from him. I have to start down this road if only to protect myself from her plans.

OK?

OK Clara.

The Gingerbread Woman

(notes, only notes)

A touch of the tragic, the comic, both there inherent in the title. Run, run as fast as you can. You can't catch me, I'm the Gingerbread Man.

Or should I say woman?

Vanity. Oh boy, such vanity.

cccclllmmm.

I have despoiled the first empty page, the endless loop of pages with six words, neatly centred.

I have started on my new journey.

cccclllllmmm.

Well, sort of started.

Let us not be pretentious about this.

Let's just get down to work and write a book, like I told my mother I was going to do.

The Gingerbread Woman meets the fox — or was it a wolf? It hardly matters. It was some predator or other, dressed slyly in the clothes of a New York stockbroker . . .

In April, New York is at its most charming, the city and the people slowly and cautiously unwrapping themselves from their winter protection. They have survived.

The sky as I remember it was wrapped in a light tissue of cloud, here a fine grey, there blue, sometimes touched with a golden light; the flower buds were bursting on the trees and then sometimes a little wind whipped round a corner, reminding everyone that maybe this reawakening was merely an illusion.

It was the suit that caught my eye first: a lanky jacket with low patch pockets and narrow trousers in mouse-brown wool that looked as soft as velvet. I presumed it was Italian, wondered how much it had cost. I took a slurp out of my fourth glass of champagne and wished that I had the figure to wear such a suit myself. I envisioned myself slinking into rooms full of glamorous people and leaning against door jambs and walls, staring enigmatically at strangers. Another world. Fingers took the tilting glass from my hand.

'You're going to spill your drink.'

Around the wrist was a gold watch with a heavy plaited gold band. It looked like it weighed several pounds. It looked like it cost several hundred.

'Did your mother never tell you not to stare?'

I started to laugh. It was really the only thing to do.

'Your suit was too much for me,' I said.

My mother, of course, wouldn't have noticed it. She would have noticed his eyes. 'Never trust men with grey eyes,' she would have said, and I would have laughed at that too. Silly me!

He took the first finger of my left hand and ran it gently down his sleeve from elbow to wrist. I had been right about the wool, it was as soft as velvet. He then let go of my finger and handed me back my glass.

'Satisfied?'

'Impressed.'

'So am I.'

At that I laughed.

He looked mildly surprised, possibly a little offended not to be taken seriously.

We stood in silence for a moment or two looking at each other.

'Shall we go?' he asked.

'Where? Why? I've only been here half an hour.'

'You can't surely be enjoying this.' He waved his hand towards the rest of the party. 'Are you with someone?'

'No.'

'So why don't we go?'

'I don't know you.'

'How bizarrely old-fashioned you are.'

He put a hand into an inside pocket and took out a card which he handed to me. James Cavan. There was a lot of other information also that I didn't bother reading. I handed him back the card.

'Thank you, Mr Cavan.'

'K'van. We pronounce it K'van.'

'And J.a.m.e.s. How do you pronounce that?'

He looked a bit cross.

'I'm only trying to be friendly.'

'I'm sorry. We just call it Cavan at home. You took me by surprise. When I'm taken by surprise, I make silly jokes.'

'Where is home?'

'Ireland. We have a county called Cavan. One of our more boring counties, I do have to say.' I finished the wine in my glass.

He said nothing, just stared at my face as I must have stared at his suit.

'Midlands, a bit flat and wet. No spectacular scenery.'

'Thank you. I'll avoid it.'

I laughed again.

'Right,' he said. 'Now that's out of the way, how about dinner?'

'My objection still stands.'

'Dinner is the time to get to know me. And for me to get to know you.'

He took hold of my elbow and began to steer me towards the door. I didn't put up much resistance.

In the elevator he spoke. 'French? Italian? Chinese?'

'It's Friday. You'll be lucky if you get a table anywhere.'

'I have ways and means. Just tell me which you'd prefer.'

'Well, if you insist . . .'

He nodded his head vigorously.

'Italian.'

He beamed. 'I thought so.'

'What does that mean?'

'It means I thought you looked like a lady who would eat Italian. A lady with romantic inclinations.'

The doors opened and we stepped out into the big hallway.

'I wouldn't count your chickens before they're hatched,' I said.

'Can you hang there for just a moment while I make a call?' Without waiting for an answer he crossed the hall to the porter's office and went in.

I could go now, I thought. Walk out the door and hop into a cab. On the other hand, I wouldn't mind a posh Italian meal. He might be fun. K'van. I wonder how long it will be before he asks me *my* name. Five minutes? An hour? Never? *Melanzane al forno*. I could eat a lot of that. If I walk out the door, what do I have in the fridge? Some yogurt and the remains of yesterday's pizza. I don't have a choice really, do I? K'van wins, hands down.

The doorbell rings, ploughing into my head, and the knocker is also being rat-tatted. That is impatience verging on bad manners. How can you write a novel if people keep interrupting you? Is it the man from Porlock? Oh haha!

Or Mother?

Better by far the man from Porlock.

After sitting slouched as I do at my table, glaring and staring into the screen, my back aches and things go crackle inside when I stand up. But I will not be deflected by anyone. I will write this book and then, having vented my spleen – not the right reason, I do know that, for writing a book – I will move on. I will write another one and then another. I will do my voyaging in my head. Words and ideas will be my baggage, my eyes will turn for a while inwards.

'Hello.'

Lar is on the doorstep, complete with dog and baggage. A slightly anxious smile on his face. Not the man from Porlock.

'Where did you say you were from?'

I beckon him in as I speak.

I pat Pansy on the head as she passes.

The telephone rings. I am having a busy afternoon.

'Near Ballycastle.'

I pick up the phone and point along the passage to the short flight of stairs to the spare bedroom.

'Hello?' This is Mother.

'Just up the stairs,' I say. 'It's the only room. Yes, Mother?'

'Are you busy, dear?'

'Yes.'

73

'That's good. I thought you might be out getting wet in the rain.'

'I did that this morning.'

'Tttt.'

I wait to hear what she has to say.

'I hope you're not doing anything too energetic.'

'Writing a novel.'

'I never know when you're telling me the truth.'

'Today I am writing a novel, maybe I won't be tomorrow. Maybe tomorrow all inspiration will have dried up.'

'All you have to do is concentrate, dear.'

'Thanks.'

'Seven-thirty, then.'

'May I bring a friend? Have you enough food?' She always has enough food to feed an army.

'I decided to ask Ivan, but he's gone to Oughterard.'

I always forget that our doctor's name is Ivan. It really doesn't suit him.

'I had forgotten that he was going away. He left at eleven-fifteen, his housekeeper said. She made him sandwiches and a flask of coffee. Chicken and cheese, brown bread.' She starts to laugh. 'She told me all that on the telephone. Two bananas and a slice of chocolate cake. He will pull down a quiet lane and eat all that and be in Oughterard by teatime.'

Sometimes my mother is very close to my heart. We both laugh together.

'Yes, of course bring someone. I have enough food. Is it someone I know?'

'No. It's a man from the North – he's staying here for a few days. Laurence McGrane. He has a dog.'

'Lovely, dear. Seven-thirty. And he can bring his dog if it behaves.'

I put down the telephone.

He is standing watching me, his bag still in his hand.

'That was my mother. We're going to have supper with her tonight. I hope you don't mind. She likes to meet new people. Saves me cooking you a meal.' I give a little laugh. 'Don't get me wrong, please. Don't misinterpret me. Bring your things upstairs and then come down and make us a cup of tea. I'm exhausted. Too many things are happening to me today.'

Without a word he turns and plods up the short flight of stairs. I bet he's regretting the decision he's made. I think I am too. Pansy seems happy enough though.

* * *

Two days.

I will stay here two days.

No more.

It was kind of her to ask me and I knew the moment I went back into that dismal hotel that I was going to accept the invitation.

Laurence stared out of the window at the gardens and the hedges just becoming green and the trees and the distant bay. At home there was nothing but the ocean. You could clamber down those twenty steps, cut into the rock by someone a long time ago, and walk straight down onto the sand. No neat hedges, no zigzag pattern of roofs glistening with the day's rain.

'This is such glory. Don't you think, Lar, that it's terribly dangerous to be so happy?'

His feet were freezing. She never seemed to feel how cold the sea really was. Now the tide was creeping in, curling and gently buffeting at their feet and ankles. Sucking the gritty sand from under them and then tossing it back as the waves moved in again.

'I don't give it a thought,' he said. 'I just take what is given to me. Day by day. What else would you expect me to do?'

'Fear,' she said. 'I fear.'

He was surprised. He had never suspected that she might have any dark thoughts. At moments like this he was always surprised at how little he knew of her. She kept secrets so well, he thought. He stared out across the sea, disturbed by the pain in her voice.

She took his arm and hugged it. 'One of the things I love about you is that you don't have any fear. I love that. I get strength from that.'

Damn, he thought, damn, damn.

He was still holding the bag in his hand. He let it fall with a thud to the floor. He wondered if she would let him use her washing machine; or was that perhaps taking advantage of her hospitality?

He went down the stairs and into the kitchen, where Pansy was lying quite at home beside the Aga. Her tail thumped gently as he came into the room. The lid of the kettle was clicking on the hot ring.

'The tea's on the shelf over the Aga,' her voice called from the next room. Clara's voice, he had to remind himself, not Caitlin's voice. Her voice was becoming muddy in his head. Though he heard it so frequently, he was no longer sure if he was hearing it correctly. Had it been lower? Higher? Softer? Had her vowels sounded longer or shorter? Had she really rolled her Rs with a slight French twang? Her voice was breaking up in his head. What did this mean?

He took the tea caddy from the shelf and put two spoons of tea into the pot. The kettle was heavy and he leaned it forward and the steaming water poured in an arc on top of the tea-leaves.

'It does not mean that I am forgetting you. It's just . . .' He tilted the kettle back again and then pushed it to one side of the hot ring.

'Just what?'

Clara was standing at the table behind him.

'I'm sorry to interrupt your conversation. I heard nothing but silence and I thought you might have dropped dead or something. Bring the pot in. I have cups and milk in here.'

Teapot in hand he followed her into the sitting room. She lay down on the sofa and pulled a rug up over her legs.

'You talk to yourself a lot,' she said. 'I've noticed that. Perhaps not yourself, but some person sitting in your head. I do too, I have to say, but I quite enjoy it. I can make myself laugh. You don't seem to enjoy it.'

There were mugs on the table and milk in a flowered jug and a plate of shortbread.

He frowned.

He poured tea into one mug and pushed it over towards her.

She held up her hand like a policeman. 'I'll wait a few minutes. I like my tea dark brown and almost solid. I bet you only put one spoon in.'

'Two.'

'I'll wait a while. Sit down.'

He sat down, slightly anxiously it seemed, on the edge of an armchair, his cup held before him as if for protection.

'Talk to me,' she said. 'I have become too self-absorbed. I spend too much time feeling sorry for myself.'

'I have nothing to say. She always spoke for me.'

'Caitlin?'

'I was brought up to keep my thoughts to myself. Figures, calculations, configurations, mathematical and geometric excavations. Those are the things I carry in my head. There aren't too many people who become excited when you talk that sort of stuff to them. "Smile at everyone and keep your mouth buttoned." My father said that once to me. That is how he has always behaved. Even, I think, with his oldest friends. No one spoke much. I have no idea what goes on in his head, or my mother's. I don't know what they say to each other when they are alone. I do have to say though that they are circumspect and kindly people.'

He took a drink of tea and put his cup down on the table. Without thinking he took a piece of shortbread and chewed at it. Glints of sugar clung to his lips.

'You could pour my tea now, please.' Her voice was gentle.

He leant forward and poured tea into her cup. She nodded as she watched the darkness of the liquid falling from the spout.

'I suppose you could say that as a family we were gutted by history.'

He pushed the mug over towards her.

'What an obnoxious thought.'

He gave a little grunting laugh at the world she had used.

'There is no way you could possibly understand.'

'You never know your luck.'

'I know my luck.'

'You met Caitlin.'

'Dancing?' She held her hands out towards him and smiled. Dressed in black, always in black.

He shook his head to dislodge the memory. 'That was her bad luck.'

'I don't suppose she thought so. Shove over the milk, would you?'

His hand was shaking as he pushed the jug across the table. She poured some into her tea and watched it swirl for a moment. 'You seem to have enjoyed great mutual happiness.'

'She might have been alive now. If,' he raised his voice, 'if only . . . if she hadn't . . . if I . . . she . . . if . . .'

'Great mutual happiness doesn't come all that often to people. Perhaps it would be better if you were to think of that, rather than keep saying "if".'

'People who haven't suffered find it easy to give advice.'

'That's quite rude, you know. Quite an uncaring attitude to have towards other people.'

'The child, my child, our child had six wee teeth. I think from time to time about that.'

'Moya? Is that what you said her name was?'

'Yes. I'm sorry, I don't mean to be rude. I have been rude to so many people over the last while. I say things without thinking – well, sometimes that's not true. Sometimes I mean to be rude. Vicious. I . . .' He suddenly smiled at her, a charming and quite lively smile. 'I was feeding her one day. We had this little silver spoon that my mother had given her, and as I put it into her mouth I heard this tiny clink. I looked into her mouth and there was this wee pearly ridge just pushing up through her lower gum. It sounds so stupid to say, but I had seldom been so excited in my life. I felt stupid with excitement. As you may have gathered, I am not given to great displays of emotion. I yelled for Caitlin and we kept putting the spoon in and in and in to the child's mouth just to hear the clink over and over again.'

There was a long silence between them. Pansy came in from the kitchen and settled herself down beside Lar, her head on his knee. He scratched at the top of her head with a finger.

'Good dog,' he said eventually.

'Why did you say gutted by history?'

'It seems to me to be true. We are a gutless people, not just my family, who don't speak, but the whole damn lot of us. We allowed ourselves to be collectively bullied. That's pretty gutless, you must admit. Shaming, when you think about it. We subscribed seriously to the "whatever you say, say nothing" philosophy. We didn't raise our voices against the unreasonable behaviour of the Unionists and now we're having a problem raising our voices against the unreasonable behaviour of the Republicans. Our voices disappeared years ago with our guts, out our backsides. Sorry.'

'What's the apology for?'

'Intemperate words.'

'Intemperate thoughts perhaps,' she said, 'but the words seem quite unexceptionable.' She took a gulp from her cup, scalding the back of her throat. She grimaced and clutched for a moment at her neck. 'We're no great shakes here either, if it comes to that.' She put the cup down on the table and looked at it with anger. 'I'm always doing that. I'm surprised I have any skin left at all, or tonsils or any of those bits and pieces in there. Actually, I don't have any tonsils. They were whipped out when I was seven. It was the fashionable thing to do in those days, whether they were causing you trouble or not. Preventative medicine. Get rid of the tonsils and the adenoids before they start acting up. Pretty nasty experience. We all went through it. A middle-class rite of passage.'

He was looking at her sombrely.

'OK,' she said, waving a hand at him. 'Glare away at me. I just don't want to hear about the North. No North in this house. I don't mind you talking about your wife, your child, your mother, your hopes and fears, your punctured dreams, but not the North. None of the gutted-by-history crap. Don't pollute my house with that. When you want to have that conversation, we'll go to the pub. Or walk in the rain.'

She pulled a key out of her pocket and pushed it across the table towards him.

'Here. Come and go as you like. I cook one meal a day. You can share it with me. About eight in the evening. Take what you like the rest of the time. You can buy the wine. I prefer a nice Rhône red and Chilean white, dry. No need to spend a fortune, but I've moved beyond plonk. Now you know.' She pushed herself out of the chair. 'The washing machine is in the little scullery behind the kitchen. Use it when you like, but try not to break it. I get very ratty when the washing machine breaks down. I'm going back to work now. I'm on page two of a novel.' She began to laugh. 'It's important that I get on to page three. You know of course about the man from Porlock?'

'No. I . . .' He looked confused.

'No importance. Merely a literary joke – or tragedy, depends which way you look at it. Settle in. Read a book. Take the dog out. Do what you will. I'll see you at twenty past seven when we will go to my mother's. If I'm late she gets anxious, starts ringing the hospitals.'

She limped out of the room. Pansy thudded her tail on the floor. Lar poured himself some more tea.

* * *

The screen is grey: the colour of white shirts and handkerchiefs that have somehow got washed in the machine with something black, a depressing colour. I must try and change it. I don't want to be depressed each time i sit down to write. I want to be filled with energy and hope that i will move from page two to page three and inexorably on until that moment comes when I will tap the words *The End* and I will sit back and feel . . . how will I feel? I don't know. Purged? Astonished? That's probably it. I will feel astonished by my persistence and by the probability that I will have come to terms once more with the upper case I. I do hope so. I really don't want to spend the rest of my life relegated in my own mind to the lower case.

It was quite early on in my stay in New York that I met him, and to begin with I was sure that the excitement that I felt every day on waking up was to do with the notion of spring in New York . . .

The Gingerbread Woman

(continued)

New York is a bizarre city, so full of contradictions – black and white, heat and chill, awful poverty and equally awful wealth, dust and drenching rain the like of which we do not suffer here, callousness and inestimable kindness. Perhaps all cities are the same, but it turned Dublin in my mind into a village with all the properties and problems of a village and the comforts always there. New York has few comforts. Perhaps that is why it is so exciting to live there, the razor's edge of life.

I have already indicated that I am a cautious person and I fell, to start off with, cautiously in love with James K'van as I will continue to call him as I need to fictionalise him in my mind now, remove his cruel reality which has left scars not just on my body, but on my heart and mind as well.

Throughout my careful and loving upbringing I had observed love to be a walk into privacy. Two people, it has always seemed to me, are far more private than one. They do not need any longer the flamboyant and sometimes corrosive fever that whirls people into close encounters and even distant encounters, exposing their pains and privacies in their search for a companion. I watched my siblings with a certain amusement, and also my friends who climbed rather than fell into love while I kept running like the Gingerbread Man, away, away. You can't catch me, I'm the Gingerbread Man. You will never catch me. I, upper case, am the Gingerbread Woman.

I am not going to write all that down, just the merry and sad tale of myself and James K'van. Foolish, I think I should say rather than merry; my years of light-hearted flirting and fucking had made me very careless. I did not recognise the danger signs because I had never had to before.

I never thought I would see him again after our dinner in the Italian restaurant. With somewhat old-fashioned punctiliousness he left me at the door of my flat in Morton Street, just north of Houston and five minutes' walk from my work. As I mentioned before, it had been lent to me by a friend called Jodie for the academic year, while she was on sabbatical leave; all I had to do was feed her cats and water the plants that filled her small backyard in earthenware pots. She was having a whale of a time in India, according to the postcards she sent from time to time, and I was teaching my course on Elizabeth Bowen, Kate O' Brien and Molly Keane.

The outside of the house was dark brown and unprepossessing, and I saw that thought pass across his face as he handed me out of the cab and then gently kissed my hand. He waited on the pavement by the cab until I had turned the key in the door and opened it into the darkened hall. I turned and waved to him and he stepped back into the cab and away he went. I hadn't discovered where it was he lived, but I presumed it was the Upper East Side somewhere.

I hardly gave him a second thought that night or the next day; in fact, by the time day three had come along I had forgotten him and for a moment did not recognise the man standing at my street door with a bunch of flowers when I got home from work. I presumed he was visiting some other person and passed him on the steps, head down, rootling in my bag for my keys.

'What a short memory you have, Clara.'

I recognised his voice at once, but had to rootle also in my mind for his name; then decided not to use the name that I came up with in case I was wrong.

'Goodness me,' I said, smiling at him. 'What a surprise.'

He held the flowers out towards me. They were startling yellow daisies.

'Are they for me?' It's amazing how stupid I can be from time to time. He didn't bother to answer. I fumbled them from his cool fingers. 'Thank you.' I laughed then. 'Daft thing. I don't think anyone has ever given me flowers before. Thank you. James.' I tried the name for size. He didn't object. That was something, anyway.

'Will you come in and have a glass of wine? I'm afraid I don't have any more serious drink.'

'I'd really like that.'

I handed him back the flowers and scooped my fingers round and round the bottom of my bag until I caught the key ring and pulled it out. 'See? It always tries to hide.'

I opened the door and stepped into the dim-lit hall. Somewhere up in the dark heights of the house someone, probably Maria Callas, was singing:

> *Ah fors'è lui che l'anima*
> *Solinga ne' tumulti*
> *Godea sovente pingere*
> *De' suoi colori occulti.*

Someone had their player on fortissimo.

I couldn't blame them. I have always been a sucker for *Traviata*. Fortissimo.

'Follow,' I said to him. I put out my hand to guide him round the bend that led to the stairs to the basement. He clutched at it as if for a moment he thought he was going to drown, and kept holding on after we had come into the light of my untidy borrowed sitting room.

'Nice,' he said, looking round.

I pulled my hand away from his fingers and went across the room to open the French doors out into the garden.

'I have a tree,' I said with pride. The leaves were just bursting on the tall ginkgo. Three sides of the yard were protected, fortress-like, by high brownstone walls with higgledy-piggledy windows, the top ones reflecting the setting sun. The fourth side had a wattle fence up against which a straggly hedge struggled to look healthy.

'Mine, all mine,' I beamed. 'Until the end of term, at any rate.'

'It's great. I really don't know this part of the world very well.'

'You weren't at NYU?'

'Harvard.'

Silly me.

> *A quell amor ch'è palpito*
> *dell'universo intero,*
> *Misterioso, altero,*
> *Croce e delizia al cor.*

The voice echoed high around the walls; like a voice in a church gaining energy and body as it beat from wall to wall.

Follie! Delirio vano e questo!

A breath of wind stirred the branches of the ginkgo. We stood in silence.

Pover donna, sola, abbandonata.

He put his hand on the back of my neck; his cool fingers lightly lay there.

In questo popoloso deserto . . .

I didn't dare move in case he took his fingers away. I felt myself stop breathing

Che appellano Parigi.

Che spero or più? Che far degg'io?

God, I thought to myself, I feel like a Victorian miss, surprised by physical pleasure. I wondered if he also was holding his breath.

Gioire! Too right, Violetta.

Someone slammed down a window and the sound was swallowed back into the inside of the house. A pigeon flapped from the tree onto one of the window sills and sat waiting hopefully for food.

I hate pigeons.

I took a deep breath. He removed his hand from my neck. My skin was burning.

'Callas,' I said.

He stepped back into the room again.

'How do you know?'

'Well, I don't really. I'm not an expert, but hers is the only voice that . . .'

'That what?'

I turned and looked at him. He was staring at me. Grey eyes, quite sombre.

'. . . takes away my breath.'

'Is that what it was?'

I nodded. 'I have white wine in the fridge. Will that be OK – or are you a spirits man?'

'Fine,' he said. 'I like to stick with wine. Only the old or the very stupid fill themselves with whiskey or gin these days.' He put out a hand and stopped me as I walked past him towards the kitchen. 'Was it really Callas that made you lose your breath?'

'Of course.'

'Strange.'

I walked on towards the kitchen, hoping that there was some white wine. I opened the fridge and presto, there it was, a bottle of Sancerre, quite respectable really.

He was just behind me. 'Strange,' he repeated.

I handed him the bottle.

'There's a corkscrew on the table. Would you be kind . . .?'

'Clara.'

'. . . enough to open it, while I get the glasses?'

He turned abruptly and went back into the sitting room. By the time I followed him with two glasses, he had pulled the cork and was standing by the window, staring out at the garden.

'I am just suggesting it is strange because I lost my breath too. Not something that I do often. In fact, it has never happened to me before.'

'Callas,' I put the glasses on the table, 'has a very potent voice.'

'No,' he said. 'It wasn't Callas.'

That's where I will stop for today.

There is something terrible about remembering, even remembering such moments of extraordinary excitement. Also there's the notion in my mind that I am really inventing all this as I put it down. I am moulding reality into fiction. Is that something that always happens? I don't know yet. I suppose I will find out.

Now that I have stopped tapping, I can hear someone in my house, something to which I am quite unused. A door being softly closed, the creak of a tap being turned on, the hum of the washing machine. Oh dear God, don't let him have broken my washing machine. My prayer for today.

I am tired in my head as well as my body. I think I will stretch out and sleep a while before a bright evening with Mother.

* * *

Lar took his clothes out of the washing machine and wondered what to do with them. The washing machine was in a lean-to at the back of the kitchen. Rain now beat on the roof and rattled on the window. A clothes-drier hung from the ceiling, but it was weighted with her clothes – trousers, shirts, pants and a couple of towels. Gingerly he let it down and felt the clothes; bone dry. They'd probably been there for days, weeks even. He began to pull them off the wooden poles and fold them up. He put them in piles on top of what looked like a deep freeze, and then he flapped and shook his own wet clothes and hung them neatly on the drier. He thought about his mother as he pulled at the collar of one of his shirts.

'Why?' he said to her.

'There is no answer to that, son. So many times down the years we have asked that question. Just keep on believing in the goodness of God.'

It was the day of the funeral and she held his clean white shirt out towards him. Ironed immaculately. Smelling of soap and fresh air.

He had shaken his head.

'Put it on, Laurence. It is respectful to look your best. Don't be letting us down, or yourself for that matter. Your father has your good shoes polished. I doubt they've seen a touch of polish since the day you bought them.'

He just sat there by the window and shook his head. Let her get on with her nonsense. He wouldn't move from this chair. Let them do their burying; he would stay here and mourn. Only he could mourn; he would not take part in their public display of sorrow. He would mourn alone.

His mother's voice was sharp when next she spoke.

'Get up this minute, Laurence, and put on your clothes! We are all waiting for you, Father Hennigan and your wife and child. And Caitlin's mother. Don't forget her. What makes you think your suffering is any greater than hers? Answer me that. You're making me very angry, son. These things all have to be done before you can be healed. You know that as well as I.'

'I don't want to be healed.'

'You don't know what you want. Now put on your clean clothes and let's go to the church.'

I did not want to be healed.

Pull the sleeves right side out, smooth the cuffs.

I still don't.

He had put on his clean clothes, of course, and had gone to the funeral and had closed his ears to the words that were spoken, and his eyes to the sorrow on the faces of the people around him.

I am the resurrection and the life saith the Lord.

Caitlin had taught him not to believe those words.

He that believeth in Me, though he were dead, yet shall he live.

Stretch the legs of the jeans, fold them neatly sideways.

And whosoever liveth and believeth in Me shall never die.

Why had she taken that security from him, so that now he could receive no comfort?

He pulled the clothes-drier up to the ceiling and twisted the rope round a hook on the wall.

So she had willed him to be comfortless without her.

Suddenly he liked that idea. He liked that notion of ruthlessness in love.

He went back into the kitchen; Pansy stretched by the Aga opened an eye and gave a thump with her tail.

'Come on, pooch,' he said. 'We'll take a walk in the rain. We'll go and get this lady some bottles of wine, just to show her that we mean well.' He pulled his anorak from the hook near the door and took the dog's lead from the pocket. 'Let's get wet. Yet again.'

*　*　*

Clara's mother was a nice lady.

She didn't kiss her daughter when they stepped into the hall, but she held her shoulder for a moment, her white fingers gauging the fragility of the bones.

She noticed him watching her and took her hand from Clara's shoulder and held it out towards him.

'You're welcome.'

'Laurence McGrane,' said Clara, in a phony Northern accent.

Her mother frowned at her. She wore a necklace of creamy pearls that swung down into the scented cleft between her breasts and the opening of a blue silk blouse.

He took her hand and shook it. 'It's very kind of you,' he

handed her a bottle of Côtes du Rhône, 'to invite me along too.'

'Divine smell,' said Clara. 'What are we having for dinner?'

'Roast beef. I do hope you're not a vegetarian. You never know with Clara's friends.'

He shook his head.

'He hasn't had a proper meal for weeks.' Clara walked on in front of them into the sitting room.

'Thank you for the wine. That was really thoughtful of you. Clara said you had a dog.'

'We left her at home.' He blushed for some reason as he spoke the words. 'Well, you know, at . . . It was too wet to bring her. She's fine. She's so pleased not to be living in the car any longer.'

They stood in the sitting room smiling somewhat foolishly at each other.

'Do sit down, Mr McGrane.' She waved her arm around the room full of chintz-covered chairs, all green and fresh; they didn't look as if anyone had sat on them ever before.

'Everyone calls me Lar.' He sat down as he spoke, facing the long window that gave onto the green of trees and lawn.

'Except his mother,' said Clara, 'who calls him Laurence. I think you could take your pick.'

'Get the poor man a drink and stop being tiresome, Clara.' She sat down beside Lar and smiled at him. 'Clara is the most tiresome of my four children.'

Lar blushed again.

'Whiskey, gin or white wine?' asked Clara.

'Well, ah, whiskey would be very nice. Thank you.'

Clara clinked and rattled in a corner of the room.

'Have you known each other long?'

Clara laughed.

'No. Just a couple of days,' he said.

'Oh.'

'Clara very kindly . . .'

'Don't let her bully you.'

Clara walked across the room and put a glass down in front of each of them.

'. . . very kindly asked me to stay with her.'

'Just for a couple of days,' said Clara. She went back across the room and poured herself a glass of wine. 'My better nature coming into play. And that is that. We will now talk of other things.'

There was a silence.

'Shoes and ships and sealing wax and—'

'Clara!'

'Sorry, Mother.'

'What have you been doing since you arrived, Laurence?'

'Nothing really. Taking the dog for walks. I'm not—'

'He's sick,' said Clara. 'In the head.'

'Clara!'

'I thought you might be able to sort him out. He needs a mother.'

'Oh, I'm sorry. Is your mother . . .?'

'Ballycastle. My mother's alive and well and living near Ballycastle.'

Clara's mother sighed.

'I think we'd better go and have our dinner,' she said.

*　*　*

It was still raining when they walked home, both close together under the umbrella.

'Your mother's nice,' he said.

'Mmmm.'

The rain pattered on the nylon arc above them and slid off onto their shoulders. The sound of water filled their ears, tumbling, splashing, running, their feet squelching through puddles. The wind blew sparkling drops across the surface of the road.

'She gets up my nose.'

'I can't think why.'

'She's *too* fucking nice! I don't like people who are all nice – it makes me feel *soooo* inadequate. And she knows me too well. Lots of parents don't know their children at all, don't even bloody want to know the realities of their children. It's too disturbing for them. But she knows everything. Well, almost everything. I do have a few secrets, but I have to fight hard to keep them. People need secrets, don't you think?'

'Perhaps.'

'Do you always sit on the fence? Say perhaps or maybe? Possibly? Is that the sort of person you are? Someone who sits all the time on fences?'

'I don't like being bullied. Your mother said—'

'I like people to answer my questions.'

'So did the Gestapo.'

She gave a little spurt of laughter and then gasped. She stopped walking for a moment and took a deep breath, her hand grasping at her side. She shook her head towards him.

'Ouch,' she said. 'Laughing is not allowed. Such a bugger.' She took his arm and they walked slowly on in silence.

By the time they reached her garden gate the moon had forced its way out from behind a cloud and everything had become silver and black, black trees dripping silver drops, silver roofs shining, and black valleys between the houses. She turned towards him and touched his face.

'Are you alive?' she asked. 'You look like a ghost.' Her fingers were icy cold.

'So do you,' he whispered.

Inside the house Pansy hearing their approach began to bark.

✳   ✳   ✳

The sheets smelled of apples.

For a few moments he wondered why and then he fell asleep and he dreamed, only maybe it wasn't really a dream, maybe he wasn't asleep only locked into recollection, his head buried in the apple-scented pillows.

She took a bite from the apple and handed it to him. It was red and shiny, like an apple in a fairy story, an apple full of wishes or poison; how did you ever know before you bit into it?

'Yuk,' she said. 'Plastic.'

He looked at it for a moment; the soft flesh was decorated by her toothmarks. He wound down the window and threw the apple across the road.

'Biodegradable,' he said.

'I doubt it.'

Away below them the golden beach curved towards a distant pier and a conglomeration of little houses; the lough was grey, but out beyond it, the sun shone on the cold blue ocean, moving like a spotlight across the waves.

He put his arm around her and pulled her towards him. Her hair was wet, her face cold. *Seeing the empty beach twenty minutes earlier, the fool had stripped off all her clothes and run straight into the water; now she was wrapped in his anorak and smelling and tasting of salt.*

'Why are we so happy? Don't be negative about it this time. Just answer me.'

'Because, darling Lar, there is absolutely no reason for us to be unhappy. We have everything that any sane person could possibly want.' *She held up her fingers in front of his face.* 'Love. A roof. Food. Work. And heavenly Moya.' *She bent each finger as she spoke each world.* 'And this lovely day of blue and gold and sea and hills just to ourselves, to smile at each other and talk about the future. It would be disgraceful if we weren't happy.'

He had to believe her; she spoke with such conviction.

'Nothing else matters. Nothing. No thing. That's where other people go wrong. They don't understand how little really matters.'

A small fishing boat butted against the incoming tide, heading for the open sea; three gulls circled round it, hoping for scraps, fish heads, mouldy bread, anything in fact that no one else wanted. She nudged at him with her wet hair, pushing it into his face, his mouth tasting the salt.

'Sweetheart,' *she whispered. He loved it when she called him sweetheart.* 'I think Moya needs a brother.'

He laughed. 'Do you want to do something about this now? Is it that urgent? I'm more than willing, even in this public place.'

'No. Hang on, don't be daft. Once my exhibition is opened. That very day, perhaps. Then we go for it. Wham. We will populate the world with beautiful people. People like us — happy, loving people. Then nothing can ever go wrong again. The world will become a perfect place because of us.'

A pillar of rain blew past down the lough, engulfing the fishing boat in a tornado of drops. He closed his eyes and pulled her against him.

'You know,' *she said, her voice muffled by his jacket,* 'we could come here in *thirty-five years' time and sit, just like this and be just as happy as we are now. I feel that. I know that.' She stretched a hand out in front of her. 'My hands will be wrinkly and covered with brown spots and you will have false teeth . . .'*

'I will not.'

'Yes, you will. I can see your teeth decaying in front of my very eyes. You never wash them. You never go to the dentist, so in thirty-five years you will have a face full of china.'

'You sound just like my mother.'

'But I will love you just the same.'

'Censorious. Judgemental.'

'Truthful.'

'Exaggerating.'

'Just wait and see. I will remind you. This day, thirty-five years, I will remind you. Thirteenth of March . . .'she did some mental arithmetic '. . . two thousand and thirty.'

'It's a date.'

Fuck it. Fuck it. Fuck everything and everyone and life and death. He opened his eyes. His pillow was wet and salty, as her hair had been. The rain had stopped and light from the street-lamps trembled through his window. Pansy breathed gently on the floor at the foot of the bed.

*   *   *

I turn on the radio.

First thing I do.

Stretch the hand out, grope grope through the books and the glass of water, the pills in their shiny wrappers.

Eat me.

Take two.

First thing, last thing, after every meal.

White, brown, tiny yellow pills, pick me ups, slow me downs, put me to sleep. Rock a bye baby on the tree top.

What I really need but haven't yet said to Doctor are get up and go pills, paint the town red pills, today is the first day of my life pills. But let's face it, he won't give them to me. When I ask for them he will say in that soothing voice of his, 'It all takes time, Clara. You must have patience. Easy does it Clara.'

Anyway the bastard is in Oughterard, murdering fish.

I think I may have to open my eyes to find the radio, to see if it is daylight, to find out if I am alive or dead. I think I am probably alive, as the act of stretching plucks painfully at my side.

'Morning, Ireland.' A familiar, scratchy voice. I have hit the right button.

'Morning, David Hanley,' I mutter back and let the sound of what is going on in this great little island invade my waking mind.

The telephone rings.

Oh God, *Morning Ireland* has just started and the telephone rings.

This is too early even for Mother.

Unless of course there is a crisis.

And I suppose that if I let it go on ringing and ringing it will wake your man upstairs – and Pansy.

Therefore I pick up the receiver and speak crossly.

'Hello.'

'Clara?'

'Who else is it likely to be?'

'Good morning.'

The doctor.

'I am about to go out on the lake and I thought I'd give you a chance to say Happy Birthday to me.'

'I am post-operative. I need my sleep.'

'I am the best judge of that. Everyone here has been up for hours.'

'So?'

'So, say Happy Birthday.'

'Mother called you Ivan.'

'That is my name.'

'I always forget.'

'I'm glad you were talking about me. That makes me feel good.'

'Only *en passant*. A mention. I had to say, "Who is Ivan?"'

She laughed.

'I must go now, my brother is hooting outside the door.'

'Is your brother an owl?'

'Certainly not.'

'Happy Birthday.'

'Thank you, Clara. Please take care of yourself.'

'Fish murderer.'

'Philanderer.'

That is that. He has gone. Nothing for it but to get up.

Good morning, Ireland.

The Gingerbread Woman

(continued)

Of course he was right. It hadn't been that voice echoing round my garden that had made me lose my breath; it was the first symptom of that disease called love. But I won't plonk those words on the page just like that; I will be more roundabout in my approach as, indeed, we were with each other.

He had telephoned the following Monday; I remember the day of the week as I had hoped that he might call over the weekend. I had in fact hung around the telephone rather like an adolescent, in the hope that he might ring.

I was just on my way out the door, almost late for my first lecture. I stumbled back into the room and grabbed the phone. 'Yes?'

'Clara.'

'I was just on my way out the door.'

'I've been at work for two hours. I was going to call before, but I didn't know what time you got up. I didn't want to frighten you out of your sleep. Have you time to talk?'

'Not now. I'll be late if I do. I'm going to have to run anyway.'

'This evening. How about this evening?'

'I can't do anything this evening. There's a young Irishwoman here from home to do a reading at Ireland House and I have to be there.'

'Why?'

'I just do. It's more or less part of my job.'

'You're putting me off.'

'No. I promise.'

'What time is this reading over?'

'About ten, but I have to take her out to eat. I really can't manage tonight.'

'I've booked a table in this great place on Brooklyn Heights.'

'I'm sorry. You'll have to take someone else, or cancel.'

'Clara . . .'

'I have to go. Give me your number – I'll ring you later in the day.'

'No. I mean . . . well, no. I'm going to be in and out all day. Clara . . .'

'No,' I said, quite firmly. 'I'm really sorry.' I was.

He put down the phone.

Well, that's that, I thought to myself as I ran across Sixth Avenue. End of that story.

It was a bit of a disastrous evening really: the writer, youngish, with windblown hair, arrived with her own group of friends. My presence was an embarrassment rather than a reassurance to her. I skulked in the background drinking red wine and wishing that I were across the river in Brooklyn Heights.

She read in a slow-fast gabble a piece about infanticide, desecration of a holy site and the wickedness of nuns. I was in the front row, so I had to keep my eyes open. I wondered what James Cavan was up to. Would he be waiting outside when I came out? If ever I got out – this woman was going to read for ever. Tumultuous applause – mainly, I thought sourly, from her friends. She bowed her tousled head again and again, then held up a hand and said that she would not be answering questions and almost ran from the room. I stood up and thanked her in absentia. I would have preferred to wring her neck.

There was nobody waiting outside Ireland House when I came out and nobody called my name as I walked home along Bleecker; nobody stood on my doorstep with a bunch of flowers. For the first time since I had come to New York I wanted to be home in Dublin. Sour bloody grapes. I kicked the furniture round a bit, ate some yogurt and went to bed.

He rang even earlier the next morning, well before my normal running out the door time. I was asleep. I was in fact dreaming – one of those odd dreams about floating and falling through colours and space. I have such dreams quite often. I don't find them frightening; somehow I know that I will never fall too far or too fast. Anyway, the bell rang in my dream and I tried to push the sound away from my ears, but it went on and on and I was forced to wake up. My room was still dark, but there was a wash of grey outside the window. *My mother is dead* was my first thought, and my heart was beating so hard when I lifted the receiver that I could hardly speak. I didn't have to.

'Clara.'

'For fuck's sake.'

'I hate women who swear.'

'Well, don't ring them in the middle of the night.'

'It's five.'

'And I suppose you've been at work for an hour.'

'Five minutes. I wanted to hear your voice. Even swearing. Swear again.'

I laughed. My mother wasn't dead and I had a feeling that this man was good news, even at five o'clock in the morning.

He laughed. We both laughed comfortably together for a moment.

'What about lunch?' he asked.

'I only have an hour between lectures. Tuesday's a bad day. I work like a slave on Tuesdays. What about dinner? I could be delightful at dinnertime.'

'Tomorrow. I'll pick you up at seven-thirty. Will it suit you to be delightful then?'

'If that's the best you can do.'

'It seems much too far away, but it is the best I can do.'

'Well, then.'

'I missed you last night.'

'What did you do?'

'Walked round Central Park banging my head against trees.'

'I hope you've bruises to show for it.'

'All over. Say my name.'

'James.'

'I like that. I love your brogue.'

'I don't have a brogue.'

'Well, whatever you call it. Say it again.'

'James.'

'And.'

'Cavan.' I gave it the full Cavan blás. 'Caaavan,' I said.

'Cool,' he said.

We both laughed again.

Here I am being agreeable before cockcrow, I thought to myself.

Then his laughter stopped. 'Yes, well, thank you,' he said formally. 'If tomorrow suits you, that's fine with me. Goodbye.'

He hung up.

Shit, I said to myself and tried to go to sleep again.

Counted sheep.

Recited verse.

> *Why can't I teach Creative Writing in Minnesota?*
> *Or better still, be poet in residence at Santa Fe?*
> *Where golden-limbed girls with a full quota*
> *Of perfect teeth lionise me, feed me, lead me astray.*
>
> *A professorship, perhaps, visiting in Ann Arbor?*
> *(Nothing too strenuous, the occasional social call)*
> *What postcards I can write, what ambitions harbour:*
> *Hawaii in the springtime, Harvard in the fall.*

Good old R. McGough again, but I didn't feel like laughing.

I sat up, punched my pillows and read a book. Gradually, pale light began to slice in through my window, radios were switched on here and there, windows were thrown open and footsteps sounded in the apartment over my head.

People in New York get up too early, I thought.

* * *

'Supposing,' Lar stuck his head round her bedroom door. She was still in her dressing-gown, hunched forward staring at the screen of her computer. She didn't seem to hear him.

'Supposing,' he repeated, 'we took the car and drove somewhere, let Pansy have a really good run. Saw some landscape. It's not raining. I'd like to see some landscape.' There was no reaction from the figure, just her fingers clicking on the keyboard.

'Sorry,' he said.

'No, no, no. Don't go. Just wait till . . .' she clicked away furiously '. . . I finish this sentence.' She turned around and smiled at him. 'I'd love a cup of tea.'

'Sure.' He went back to the kitchen and put on the kettle.

'Odd bird,' he said to Pansy. She wagged her tail. He was embraced by the homeliness of the place, the murmuring kettle, the smell of food, the dog stretched by the Aga, her tail thumping on the floor. A clock on the wall ticked and water dripped from the cold tap. I must mend that for her, he thought. Cups, plates, jugs and bowls jumbled together on shelves, and jars filled with jam and fruit and pickled vegetables – pink, red, orange and yellow lined the walls. Odd bird.

I never wanted to leave my home, I never wanted to go further than down the road, perhaps around two loughs to the brown and grey mountains of Donegal.

Would I ever have taken her, as I had promised, to see the cities of Europe? I rather doubt it. I would have made excuses on and on until her energy would have leached away.

Yet here is this odd bird wanting to leave all this and go round the world.

Maybe women have itchy feet, always wanting to find out what's around the next corner. I hate the next corner. Death may again be waiting there. Hate may be waiting there.

'Where's my tea?'

She was standing beside him, barefoot, clutching her dressing-gown round her – looking, he thought, like a rather badly wrapped parcel.

'I'm so glad you came in at that moment. I was becoming

turgid in my brain.' He said to her.

She sighed. 'It happens to me all the time.'

The lid of the kettle was clattering. She went over and moved it off the hot plate.

'Let's have coffee instead? I don't feel like tea any more. How about you?'

'Either will do me.'

'Have you had breakfast?'

He nodded.

She shovelled three large spoonfuls of coffee into the coffee-pot and poured the boiling water onto them.

'Sit down. I hate people hovering.'

'I didn't mean to disturb you.'

'I'd have stopped quite soon anyway. I loathe the day arriving and me not being ready to cope with it. It is difficult to cope with crises in a dressing-gown. I hate answering the door to my mother at ten-thirty in my dressing-gown. I become speechless.'

He didn't believe that, but he said nothing.

'Yes,' she said after a long time. 'That would be a nice thing to do. I can't walk for miles but I will bring a book.' She pressed down the plunger in the coffee-pot. She turned and grinned at him. 'Like to see my scar?'

He felt himself going bright red.

'No . . I . . . No . . .'

She laughed.

'You are an idiot. The only person I show my scar to is my doctor. It's terribly nasty-looking. It's really lucky I'm not a belly dancer. There.' She pushed a mug towards him. 'I'm taking mine to the bath. I won't be long. If we dilly and dally it will start to rain or something will happen to stop us going. I'm really looking forward to this.' She shuffled from the room clutching her coffee in one hand and her dressing-gown in the other.

* * *

'You must admit it's beautiful.'

They sat on a low stone bridge and Pansy in ecstasies of joy ran nose to the ground in huge circles around them, whimpering with pleasure. Over and back she went across a brown stream that ran down the hillside, under the bridge and on across a wide stretch of valley. There was no sign of human life; just a few leaning poles indicated that somewhere, someone was receiving electricity. High above the hill a hawk hovered, its wings barely moving.

Lar thought of the Glens of Antrim. 'It's OK.'

'I don't mean the landscape. I mean,' she pointed up towards the bird, 'up there. Waiting to kill something. Watching out for some infinitesimal movement. Bird or animal. Something vulnerable — alive and vulnerable. I find that very exciting, just that notion that death can come — wham — like that, falling from the sky.'

He opened his mouth to say something, but found he couldn't. He wanted to scream at her, perhaps even to attack her with his clenched fists, thumping and thumping, making her cry out and bleed. Instead he turned and slithered down from the road to the edge of the stream, jumped across it, trailing one foot into a swirling pool as he went and then set off at speed across the valley, bounding and stumbling from tussock to tussock, dodging the whinbushes and the bog holes as he went. Pansy turned and raced after him.

Lar could hear Clara's voice calling him as he ran. 'Hey, hey, hey!'

He ran until a stitch in his side became too painful for him to continue, then he stood heaving in and out great gouts of air and wiping the sweat from his face with the sleeve of his coat. He was standing on the lip of the valley and down below him stretched fields and trees, little outcrops of rock, here and there a dark roof and away in the distance the curve of the bay and the thickening of the air around it that indicated the city. Here it felt to him that he stood in no man's land.

Caitlin stood beside him. There was no longer any blue left in the sky and the wind was quite cold. He put his arm around her and they stood in silence looking down at the sprawling lough.

'Wouldn't it be awful to think that we might never see that again?' she said. Just think of all those people who were forced away from here by poverty and hunger and were never able to come back. It probably hasn't changed all that much, you know. They'd probably recognise it, even after a hundred years. There's not too many places you can say that about.'

'It's only a matter of time. The bungalows are on the march.'

She punched at him gently. 'I prefer my notion. There are places that remain untouched, they always will. I have a great plan in my head for a series of paintings about the three north-western loughs, to do with light and dark and space. I'd like to be able to tell you exactly what I have in my head, but I feel if I talk about it, I may lose it.' She looked at him almost apologetically.

'That's all right, love.'

'I want to start work on this as soon as possible. When this exhibition is over, I can throw Moya in the back of the car and we can both come over here on good days. I can spancel her like a wee goat and I can try and work out exactly what I want to do. That's my plan. And I'll think of you in your stuffy classroom.'

'Thank you. And you and the child will probably get colds, rheumatism and chilblains.'

'She will have to suffer for her mother's art.'

She took his arm and they walked towards the car.

'Oh darling, I have to go to Belfast tomorrow, to bring up the rest of the pictures. It's your light day, isn't it? Can I leave Moy with you from lunchtime on? I should be back about six.'

'Not tomorrow, I'm afraid. The mocks are starting and there's going to be panic all over the place. I'm invigilating most of the day. I'm sorry. Why don't you ask Mother?'

'No, it's all right. I'll bring her. No problem. Your mother's so kind, but no . . . I'll bring her. She's no bother. Her first trip to the Smoke.'

If, ififififif.

No point.

Below him, Dublin smoked and smouldered in the sun.

Lar turned and looked back along the valley; there was no sign of Clara. He wasn't even quite sure where the little bridge was, but he presumed that if he followed the stream he would eventually come to it. He began to trudge, Pansy now more subdued following him closely.

I could have swapped my invigilation with Gerry. How many times had he said those words to himself?

He thought of the hawk in the sky, watching. He thought of the man who had been up on the hillside watching, quite still, behind a rock, waiting for the military vehicle to come along. Happiness in his heart, perhaps. Was there happiness in the heart of the hovering hawk? Probably not. Routine food-gathering operation.

I could have swapped my invigilation with Gerry. I could have gone home and taken the child from Caitlin's arms as she was about to strap her into the car seat. 'Who do you love, baby? Who's Daddy's girl?' I could have said as we stood and waved goodbye. I could have kissed Caitlin, blown warm air into her ear. 'Drive carefully. Love you, see you at suppertime.' Those seconds might have saved her life, both their lives. Or maybe they were meant to die. Part of some grand plan – God's plan, as his mother believed.

And the man who pushed the plunger, pressed the button, whatever the hell it was he did, was he also part of the grand plan? Was it ordered somewhere that he should take his mind off the road for a second or two, close his eyes to clear away some recollection that was disturbing him? Did he get a sudden cramp in his leg that he had to attend to? Was his mind for a moment on his girl, the sound of her voice, the taste of her inside thigh? How had he not noticed the truck slow down to let the little red car hurry past?

He could see now the rough grey stones of the bridge and the figure of Clara sitting beside it. The hawk was no longer visible in the sky.

The odd thing, one of the soldiers had said afterwards at the inquest, was that though the explosion had blown the car apart, the tape machine had continued to play; as the men had jumped from the truck and run towards the wreckage, they could hear the voice of a man singing: 'Old Macdonald had a farm, ee i ee i o. And on that farm he . . .'

Clara waved at him; he pretended not to see. Pansy gave a friendly bark and ran up the hill towards her.

Over and over the scene he had gone in his imagination, over and over, different aspects, different camera angles, picking the scab off the wound each time it seemed like the pain might be lessening.

She would have been singing too, he thought, as she passed the truck, with a little wave of her hand. 'With an oink oink here and an oink oink there, here an oink, there an . . .'

This place had a similar feel to it; the stone bridge, the stony hillside above, the silence. Up the hill and over the man must have started to run as his hand left the plunger, not waiting to see the devastation, ducking, dodging, running behind the rocks to the safety of the getaway car on the other side of the hill.

'Old Macdonald had a farm . . .'

'Yoo hoo!'

He had to hear that. He looked towards her and lifted his hand in greeting.

'What the fuck was all that about?'

The words came bouncing down the valley towards him, like a small avalanche of stones.

She must have seen the look on his face then, because she shut up. She struggled to her feet and turned away, looking back the way they had come along the black snaking road, leaning with one hand on the granite cap stone of the bridge, with the other scratching the top of Pansy's head.

He was panting and hot by the time he scrambled up from

the stream to the road, sweat running from his hairline down the side of his face.

'I'm sorry,' she said. 'I said something, didn't I?'

He pulled a handkerchief from his pocket and rubbed carefully at each side of his face.

'I have tried to work out what it could have been. Mother always says that I speak before I think. It's quite difficult to know what you can or can't say when you hardly know a person, but whatever it was, I'm sorry.'

She put her hand on his arm.

He shook his head.

'You said nothing – it's not you, it's me. I sometimes lose it.' He thought for a moment. 'It was the bird really. That,' he pointed upwards, 'hawk. I just . . .'

She squeezed his arm.

'Let's go. We've had enough country air for one day.'

*　*　*

That was good and bad.

Good: the mountainy air, quite warm, unpolluted, startling to the skin. I sat there by that little bridge feeling my skin, face, neck, hands being invigorated by the touch of that air. If I had been on my own, even post-operative, I might well have stripped off and sat there, staring up at that hawk and allowed my entire body to receive the therapy so simply offered. In other and less complicated terms I actually felt quite happy; an emotion I had thought I might never feel again.

I must get out and about more.

Bad: the reaction of that man to something I said. I felt such despair as I watched him running along the valley, looking like someone bent on self-destruction. I thought, how grim to be stuck here in this idyllic spot with a corpse and a howling dog, no one for miles to rescue me, only the hawk whose hovering now became quite sinister in my mind. I tried to think of a Roger McGough poem to say out loud to myself, but I couldn't. I just watched him as he ran until he came to what seemed to be an edge and then he stopped running and stood looking out over the sky and floating clouds. At least he didn't seem to be going to do anything idiotic so I closed my eyes then and let happiness seep into my bones.

I must tell the doctor about that experience; it costs less than pills and potions.

I don't think we spoke much on the drive home. To tell the truth, I was afraid that I might again say something that would upset Lar, and he was sunk in some misery of his own. I wondered if he would tell me what it was; I also wondered if I wanted to know.

As we came in the door he gave me a little push towards my room and said, 'I'm in charge for the rest of the day. I'm going to shop and cook us a meal. You go and do whatever it is you do in there.'

Good feeling, someone else in charge. Only temporarily, though. Oh yes, only temporarily.

Yes

The Gingerbread Woman

(continued)

Yes. He rang the bell at seven-thirty, and I was ready waiting, feeling like a child going off on a treat, part apprehensive, part joyful. His arms were full of parcels and my heart sank momentarily. He's going to expect me to cook, I thought. Surprise, surprise! I was going to say something sarcastic, but before I could even open my mouth, he leant towards me and brushed my cheek with his.

'I've been so scared,' he said. 'I thought maybe my memory was playing games with me, but it wasn't. You're just as beautiful as I thought you were.'

I allowed him through the door without saying anything.

'I do hope you won't be angry with me. I dropped into Zabar's on the way here and I have everything. Everything. I am going to make a feast for you.'

He clumped down the stairs behind me, the bags rustling and clinking as he moved. I still didn't speak. I felt sarcastic in my head though. Inside my door he lowered the parcels to the floor and took hold of me. He kissed the back of my neck and then turned me round towards him.

'It's been so long. I honestly tortured myself with the notion that I would have forgotten what you looked like. I just knew I wanted you to myself. I didn't want to share a single one of your smiles with anyone else. I wanted so much to be alone with you. No world to get in the way. Oh Clara.'

I wondered in my irritation who had written his script, but then he kissed me and that was that. I didn't care any longer where we ate, what we ate or even whether we ate at all.

'You haven't said hello, good evening, or even nice to see you,' he said after quite a long time.

'Hello. Good evening. Nice to see you.'

'Really?'

'Really.'

He let go of me and rummaged in the bags. 'I have everything,' he said, pulling things out of the bags like a conjuror takes rabbits and ribbons from a hat. 'Candles – you can deal with them. That will be your only chore. Champagne – Californian. I hope that's OK with you. A nice Côtes du Rhône. Trust me. Pâté, pie, salads and *mousse au chocolat*, some Brie and a neat box of chêvres. I presume you have coffee and here's a bottle of brandy. What do you say?'

'Cool.'

He picked up the champagne and began to fiddle with the wire. 'I love this moment,' he said. I fetched two glases and held them out towards him. 'This moment of expectation, before anything or nothing happens. Like the moment before the curtain goes up in the theatre or as the conductor raises his baton and waits for silence from the audience. Sublime expectation.'

The cork popped in a civilised fashion into his hand and he filled the two glasses, the wine foaming over the rim and down over the fingers of my right hand.

We swigged our first glasses.

'Skoal!'

'Sláinte!'

'Santé!'

'Mud in your eye!'

'Gezundheit!'

I laughed. 'Nah. That won't do.'

He took my hand. 'Clara.'

'Yes?'

'Clara.'

'Yes. Yes. Yes.'

He kissed my fingers one by one, licked the champagne from them, smiled. 'I have to tell you something,' he whispered.

'Be my guest.'

'I am forty-two. I no longer like to make love on the floor, or up against a wall, I prefer a bed. Have you a bed?'

'Now?'

'Oh, I think so, don't you? Food tastes so much better after love. This will be the perfect hors d'oeuvre. After that you can light the candles and I will make the food, and after that . . .'

'After that?'

'Who knows, darling Clara.'

I had dressed carefully for going out and he undressed me just as carefully and I never asked him all those questions that should be asked. I never even thought about such questions. I thought about nothing and the lights came on in the street and shone down, silver into my bedroom, and his eyes glittered in the silver light, I thought from time to time, when I was able to think, that maybe he was a god. We moved together from silver to black and back to silver again.

We moved.

I don't remember what we talked about later on, by the light of twelve candles. I had pulled the table over to the window, so that we could look out at the tree and the shadows of the branches in the light from the street-lamps. I remember that and the twelve candles and the reflection of the candles in his eyes, flickering as he leant towards me. When I come to flesh out these notes, I will have to invent that conversation. The little laughs, the hints of intimacy, questions, answers, the silences that seemed at the time to mean so much. The small misunderstandings of pauses and glances, the lies. I do have to say lies; the lies had to be there, either spoken or by implication and I, who had always prided myself on my capacity to ferret out the truth when faced with another human being, allowed myself to be bamboozled.

I made coffee and we sat by the window, our hands clasped across the table among the litter of dishes and glasses. The little wall clock in the kitchen pinged eleven. He glanced down at his watch.

'Oh my Gaaad!' Disentangling our hands, he stood up.

'What?'

'I have to go.'

He began to move towards the bedroom.

'But why? It's only eleven. Why do you have to go so soon? Why can't you stay the night?'

I followed him across the room.

He began to dress, socks first and then his pale creamy shirt. 'Darling, I am so sorry. There is nothing I can do. My mother is staying with me. I should have had dinner with her tonight. Boy, was she peevish when I said I couldn't.' He laughed at the thought, his fingers quickly buttoning small pearly buttons as he spoke. 'She likes to be cosseted. She wants my full attention when she comes up. God, all the time really. A spoilt woman. Anyway . . . anywaaay I promised her that I would be back by eleven-thirty. She likes a whiskey and a few words before she goes to bed.' He put his tie around his neck and leant forward and kissed my cheek. 'I really hoped that you would understand. I'm sorry, my darling, I should have said this earlier, but I wasn't sure . . . I thought you might have shown me the door.' He knotted the tie and looked past me towards the mirror, shifting his head from side to side to make sure it was neatly centred.

I remember all that quite clearly. His socks were coffee-coloured silk.

'That's all right,' I said. 'Mothers can be such a nuisance.'

The look he gave me was almost grateful. He pulled on his trousers and zipped them up. I picked his shoes up from the floor and handed them to him.

'Thanks.'

'How long is your mother staying with you?'

He shrugged.

'She is a law unto herself, but not to worry. As long as I obey the Cinderella rule we don't have a problem.'

He took a comb from his pocket and frowned at himself in the mirror as he combed his hair, then he put on his jacket. He turned away from the mirror and took hold of my shoulders.

'One day you'll meet her and you can see for yourself how formidable she is. Not just yet, not yet, sweetie. We all need time to work this out.' He kissed my forehead gently. 'I think

I'm falling in love with you. I think this may be real. I don't want Mother in there laying about her. Understand – please do that for me. I must fly. I'll call you tomorrow.'

'Give me your mobile number.'

'Never use the things. Who wants to carry all that trouble round with them? Don't bother to come to the door.'

He was gone and I was there alone with twelve flickering candles and the clearing up.

Povera donna, sola, abbandonata,

I sang as I carried the plates into the kitchen.

In questo popoloso deserto
Che appellano Parigi.

One of the great things about New York is the fact that every time you turn on a hot tap, hot water comes pouring out, unlike even the best-regulated taps at home. I stood surrounded by steam and let rip.

Che spero or più? Che far degg'io?
Gioir!

Pity I have a voice like a crow, except in my head. (This is, of course, self-indulgent nonsense and won't get into the book when I come to write it.)

Gioir!

        ✳   ✳   ✳

Lar drove down the hill to Dalkey village and parked his car in the station car park. Pansy lay stretched on the back seat worn out after her run on the mountainside. She merely twitched an ear when he got out of the car. Lar strolled down the street wondering where he might find a chicken. He was able to cook a chicken; chickens, after all, almost cook themselves. He had learnt that from Caitlin.

There were restaurants to left and right. Maybe that's what he should do, take her to a restaurant. He stopped to read a menu.

'You are Laurence, aren't you?' It was Clara's mother.

'Hello. Good afternoon. Yes, it's Laurence.'

'Has Clara sent you to do the shopping?'

'Well, I said I'd cook tonight, but now I wonder should I take her out. Perhaps you could . . . Mrs . . . Ah . . .'

She laughed.

'Don't tell me you don't know her name. My name. Our name.'

He felt his face going red.

'I . . .'

'I don't mean to tease you. It's so like Clara to ignore the essentials, like names. She doesn't think they matter. Barry. How do you do?'

She held her hand out towards him.

He shook it.

'How do you do, Mrs Barry?'

'I was thinking of going in here for a cup of coffee. They do quite good coffee. Real coffee. Have you time to join me? It would be so nice if you had.'

'Thank you. I – thank you.'

He held the door open for her and then followed her in.

'I'm supposed to be looking for a chicken.'

'Lots of time for that later.'

They sat down. She wore gloves and he watched her pull

them carefully off, finger by finger, and put them into her bag. 'I always leave gloves behind if I don't take care. It can become expensive.'

Her hands were white, the fingers long and well cared for, the nails well shaped and shining, not what he would have expected from the passionate jam-maker and bottler that Clara had described. Not a bit like his own mother. His own mother was admirable, he thought, lovable indeed, but always seemed to be a shadowy figure outside her own four walls, rather like a snail that has temporarily lost its shell and is afraid of being stepped on. That thought made him smile.

She was saying something.

'Sorry, what did you say? I was . . .'

'A million miles away. Coffee? Or would you rather have tea? They do a good cappuccino here. That's quite hard to find. Unless, of course, you happen to be in Italy. That's what I will have.'

'Yes,' he said. 'That would be great.'

She called over to the girl behind the counter, her voice slightly imperious. The girl nodded.

'How splendid to have bumped into you like this. I have been thinking about you. I am a very inquisitive old lady — a nosy-parker, I think Clara would call me. She has been very ill, you know. She needs looking after.'

'Yes. She told me.'

'I'm sure she didn't tell you quite how ill. She hasn't told me either. She's either protecting her privacy or my anxiety, perhaps a bit of both. Thank you, Maire. Just what we need.' She smiled at the girl who had placed two foaming cups on the table. 'My afternoon fix! Cappuccino and gossip, every afternoon at four-thirty. Maire knows everything that goes on in this village.' She took a sip from her coffee and then licked the foam from her lips with her neat pink tongue. 'Now tell me about yourself. You didn't get much chance last night.'

'Clara's being very kind to me.'

'Yes, yes, yes.' Her voice was impatient. 'Clara's very kind to a lot of people, but not always to herself. I don't need to know about Clara. I need to know about you.'

Silence lay between them. She leant across the table and poked his arm with a finger.

'There isn't much to know.'

'Why did she say that thing about you being sick in the head?'

'I don't know. Maybe that's her assessment of me. I am a bit depressed. That's all.'

'Where did you meet?'

'On Killiney Hill. I was walking my dog and I saw her. I . . . ah . . . thought that she was a bit near the edge and it gave me a sort of queer feeling, so I asked her to take care.'

Mrs Barry nodded.

'Anyway, she offered me a bed for a couple of days because she thought I was depressed and the hotel wasn't quite the right place. There's no more to it than that, just in case you were . . .'

She shook her head.

'My wife died two years ago and I just had to get away. And our baby. Little . . .' he paused.

She placed her cool hand over his on the table and let it stay there.

'Moya. She was called after my wife's mother. Things have just been building up, inside my head. Filling my head. I couldn't stick it another moment.'

'What happened them?'

He looked at her for a long time, wondering what to say. She kept her hand on his.

'I don't think I can tell you.'

She sighed.

'Maybe Clara's right. Maybe you are sick in the head.'

'Because I want my privacies? What's sick about that?'

'Because you want to trap pain and keep it in your head, feed it and let it grow until there's no room in there for anything else.'

'That's my affair.'

'Not really. It is my view that we have to keep ourselves reasonably fit and well in order to fulfil our obligations to the rest of the world — well, to the people who love and trust us, anyway.'

He picked up his spoon and stirred his coffee. She looked disapproving.

'You shouldn't stir cappuccino,' she said.

He went on stirring.

'It's a very Protestant point of view,' he said after a long silence.

'I don't think so. It's a common-sense point of view. I am a very common-sense sort of person as I am sure Clara will have told you. We have obligations, you know, to the people who love us, if not to society. Even the most underprivileged people have obligations, loyalties.'

He wondered about that. His mother used to talk about

'obligements'; he had never really understood the meaning of that word.

He removed his hand from under hers and sipped at his coffee. She was right – you shouldn't stir cappuccino. He made a slight grimace. She smiled suddenly. Her smile was very sweet.

'They were blown up.' He spoke very fast because he hated to say the words. He shut his eyes so that he couldn't see what he supposed was going to be sympathy in her face. He spoke faster and faster so that she couldn't possibly get a word in edgeways, and so that he could finish the recitation in double-quick time.

'I couldn't go with her that day. I couldn't even keep the child. I was invigilating. I'm a teacher. I really was invigilating. It wasn't an excuse to get out of minding the child. We all had to do our stint, you know. I wasn't even there to wave them goodbye. I would have been sitting up at that desk correcting papers and taking the odd turn round the room just to make sure that no hanky panky was going on. That wasn't likely, but you never know, you have to keep your eyes peeled.

'She used to drive quite fast. She had this little red VW – nippy, the child strapped into the back. She always strapped the child into her wee seat and played tapes for her. Moya was good in the car. Happy. She liked the movement and stuff flashing past the windows. I like to believe she was asleep, what with the motion of the car and the music. Anyway, Caitlin must have zipped past this army truck and got to the bridge just as they blew it up. That's all. A little humpy bridge over a mountain stream. This stony hill, just here.' He pushed his cup to the left and drew the pattern of the stream with a finger on the cloth. He laid his spoon over the invisible stream to indicate the bridge.

A few drops of milky coffee splattered on the cloth.

'The truck was blown off the road, just sideways, into the ditch. Not overturned or anything like that. None of the men were hurt and they ran . . . they said they didn't even think of snipers or anything. They ran, but there wasn't anything they could do. One man said the tape was still playing. "Old Macdonald had a farm." '

'Laurence . . .'

'There is no point in saying you're sorry. That's what everyone has said. Sorry, sorry. The whole world was screaming sorry at me. Even the bastards who killed them said they were sorry. They said I must understand that they deplored all the deaths of innocent civilians, but they weren't to blame. It was the fault—'

'You don't have to tell me. I know what they said.'

'I hate. I have hated now for two years and I can't rid myself of that burden. I hate myself too. I even hate the children I teach.' He looked up at her and gave an angry grin. 'See what happens when you invite unknown men to have coffee with you.'

'It's risky,' she agreed.

'I hate.' He repeated the words quite loudly and the girl at the counter looked over towards them. Mrs Barry lifted two fingers to indicate more coffee.

'Black,' she said aloud across the room. He didn't seem to notice.

'The police came for me at the school and I thought she'd had an accident. Christ no, I kept saying to myself. Driving too fast. I always told her to drive carefully. "What's she done?

What's she done? Is she all right? Is the baby . . .? Is the . . .?" I must have been muttering out aloud. She liked to take dodgy little risks; nip round a corner here, pass a brute there. I used to hold onto my seat and hope for the best, but I never expected her to have an accident. Never. She drove well. Fast, yes, but well. I didn't hear what they were saying, until one of them took me by the arm and said, "You're not getting the drift," and the headmaster said, "Stop blethering, Lar, and listen to what the man is telling you." Then I heard. That was the moment I heard. In his study. It was a blustery day, Mrs Barry, and I could hear the wind in his chimney. A very old-fashioned sound, that. Like a fucking banshee. I'm sorry.'

'That's all right,' she said.

'I heard. She nipped past an army truck, they told me and landed on this bridge.' He picked up his spoon again and twiddled it in his fingers for a moment and then put it back down in the saucer. 'Just as this bugger shoved a plunger.' He was silent for a moment. 'I had to identify them, Mrs Barry. At least then I knew they were dead. This was no f . . . joke. No one was playing a joke on me. I knew that then for sure. I don't suppose you can imagine what it's like to identify a ten-month-old baby who's been . . .'

She put out a hand and touched his arm.

'Just stop a minute,' she said. 'Take a breath.'

She sounded like a bloody schoolteacher, he thought. He took a breath.

'That's better,' she said.

'My wife and child died for Ireland.'

'Laurence . . .'

'So that Ireland should be free from the centre to the sea and hurrah for liberty says the Shan Van Vocht.'

'When did this terrible thing happen?'

'Two years ago. It was a lovely spring day, just like today. A peace and love kind of a day. The kind of a day when you get up in the morning and say, "It's great to be alive." I don't want you to say anything, Mrs Barry.'

She shook her head.

'I don't want any of your decent kindly thoughts to rub off on me. I want to be allowed to hate in peace. I think that one of the reasons I liked Clara from the word go was the fact that I thought at that moment when I saw her first that she was going to do the thing that I had never yet had the guts to do. Get out.'

'Drink your coffee before it gets cold.'

Obediently, he picked up the cup and took a quick sip.

'Have you told Clara all this?'

'No.'

She looked relieved.

'I don't tell anyone. As I said before, I like my privacies. I don't want to rationalise, or share pain. I don't want to heal, because there is always the possibility that that might mean forgetting. I want to remember every tiny detail and I want to hate. That's all.' He put the cup down. 'I don't know why I spoke to you. I wish I hadn't. That's no reflection on you. Please believe that.' He pushed his chair back and stood up. 'Thanks for the coffee. I'm sorry if you think I'm a selfish jerk.'

'There is no need to tell Clara all this. I would prefer it if you were to leave her unburdened, for the time being anyway.'

'I have no intention of burdening her — and just in case you're thinking about all the rest of that stuff that goes on between men and women, don't worry. I like her, but she's not my cup of tea. Never would be even if I were . . .'

'Were?'

'Free.'

He nodded and turned towards the door.

She watched him move through the dark café. As he got to the door she called after him, 'There's a butcher halfway along the street on the right. He sells free-range chickens.'

* * *

I can smell chicken cooking.

I wonder if he knows how to use an Aga? I would hate my chicken to be charred.

I will resist going out and offering to give him a hand. Apart from the fact that I wouldn't want to humiliate him, I feel he owes me a meal. I am saving him from himself. A fact I do not think he is aware of.

I think it is probably pulp nonsense that I am writing, but I will finish it through, my notes anyway so that I can look with a certain coolness at how I allowed myself to be duped and then . . . and then . . . what word should I use? The one that springs to mind is 'destroyed', but that is way over the top. 'Damaged' would be more accurate. And of course there is the matter of my future, my immortality, only I can secure that now.

Does it matter anyway?

Immortality.

Needy vanity.

Anyway I want to cure myself — not just the bodily wounds, but those in my heart and soul. My belly will always carry a scar, but I see no reason why I should tolerate them in any other part of my being.

I know what advice my mother would give if I were to broach such thoughts.

Exercise in moderation, given my post-operative condition.

Good healthy food.

Lots of sleep.

Sea bathing.

Work.

Getting out and seeing your friends.

No introspection.

I've had all this advice before. I've also heard it being given to others. My sisters. My nieces.

It's not advice she gives to men.

She never mentions God.

She herself has some brisk kind of relationship with God; consisting mainly I think of her telling Him where He's going wrong, but she doesn't expect any of us either to believe or disbelieve. I think she thinks that she is better at looking after us than He could ever possibly be.

'No man is worth breaking your heart over.' I heard her say that to my sister Rosie once ages ago, when Rosie had just been dumped by some rugby-playing jerk. 'Particularly not *that* man!' I misguidedly put in my tuppenceworth — at which moment they both turned and ate the face off me! That's what you get for involving yourself in family life.

No introspection.

'You think too much, Clara.' She says that quite frequently. I exasperate her quite frequently.

Probably not as often as she exasperates me. Oh botheration, what am I doing sitting here thinking about my mother?

I really want to work out the first moment when a wisp of doubt crossed my mind.

As the weeks went past . . .

The Gingerbread Woman

(continued)

As the weeks went past and spring turned into delicious early summer, I slowly closed all my faculties down. My life shrank to work, and my meetings with James. Three evenings a week he came to my apartment, laden with bags and bottles and flowers. I bought the candles. That was all I was expected to do. Twelve candles – red, green, white, yellow, sometimes even gold or silver. He became like an excited child when he entered my door; the trappings of New York tumbled from his shoulders as he unpacked his picnics, opening waxed paper parcels, laying the delicious prizes that he had brought on the table in front of me. We ate on those evenings food from Japan, Mexico, China, Italy, France, Spain, Greece, Israel and India. We became connoisseurs of wine from all over the world. From seven-thirty to eleven three nights a week we became drunk with wine and laughter and love. He told me all about his life – school, Harvard, his father's fairly recent death in a motor accident and his subsequent close and almost stifling relationship with his mother.

His father's death was still too recent for him to try to disentangle himself from her. She still needed, he told me, his constant attention, his presence, the reassurance of his total love. I understood. I promised him that I did. I really believed that I understood. As I mentioned, my faculties were closing down.

One day, round about the end of May, one of my colleagues, a woman called Sophie with whom I had been pretty friendly, bounced into my office, just as I was about to go home.

It was a James day.

My week by then went something like this: Jamesday, Tuesday, Jamesday, Jamesday, Friday. Most weekends he had to spend with his mother at her home in Connecticut, but he would ring me from time to time, when he was alone, usually late at night.

'Hi Clara,' she said.

'Hi.'

'Have you dropped off the edge of the world?'

I think I must have gone a little red. 'What do you mean?'

'We only see you in the corridors these days. Have we done something to upset you?'

'No. What makes you think that? You've done nothing.'

'You've been notable by your absence. We thought we'd take you out to dinner tonight, and assure you that we love you and miss your presence. What do you say?'

'I can't, I'm really sorry. I've . . .'

'A date?'

'Yes.'

'Bring him with you. We'd love to meet him – check out his suitability. I take it he's not a Faculty member, otherwise we'd know all about it.'

'I can't tonight, but let me talk to him. It'd be great to meet some other time.'

'Come on, baby, don't be shy about this. We'll be at La Bohème from eight on. Drag the guy around and let's have a look at him. You don't need to stay, just have a glass of wine if you like.'

'Not tonight. Maybe next week. I'll talk to him about it. He doesn't like going out much.'

'OK, whatever. Just don't forget that the world exists. It's not one of those secret things, is it? You're not involved in a third-party sort of situation, are you?'

I laughed. The confidence in my laughter must have reassured her.

'Nothing like that at all, I promise. Just getting to know each other.'

She looked relieved.

'Great. There are some real jerks around.'

'As if I didn't know.'

'Food!'

Interruption. Dislocation of thought.

'Clara?'

Yes yes yes.

'Yes.'

Click. Double click.

Click.

cccccllllmm.

'Coming.'

*　*　*

132

'If I were rich . . .'

The chicken had been remarkably good and all the little accoutrements that went with it, herby, garlicky, were better than she could have managed. In fact, if the truth were to be told, she'd probably have settled for a ham sandwich and a bowl of soup.

'If you were rich?' Lar prompted her.

'I would have a wonderful Italian housekeeper, who would cook me fattening, comforting meals and iron my sheets. "Signora Clara," she would call me, and she would always be there, cherishing me.'

'A slave.'

She giggled.

'Perhaps. We would both love each other though. She would manifest her love through the medium of food and brushing my hair. I love that, someone brushing my hair, until it crackles with electricity and flies out from my head in a big swirl. And I would manifest my love for her by saying things to her like, "Oh Caterina, how could I ever live without you?" '

'It seems to me that she wouldn't come out of the arrangement very well.'

'It's just a dream.'

'Not much of a dream.'

'Maybe not. It gives me the odd little chuckle of pleasure though. I sometimes feel I'm going to see the very woman passing me in the street one day. When I do I will shout, "I need you," at her and see what happens.'

'I met your mother in the street. In Dalkey, when I was doing the shopping.'

'And you recognised her?'

'Well, she recognised me really. She bought me a cup of coffee. Two cups.'

'What did you talk about?'

'Just this and that. She's a very nice lady. She could brush your hair for you.'

'She used to,' Clara told him. 'I ran away from that a long time ago. I bet she winkled your entire life history out of you, the half-hour version.'

'Sort of.'

'She has an insatiable curiosity about people. I have to take a lot of care not to let slip my secrets.'

He nodded. Too right, he thought.

'That was really good, Lar. Where did you learn to cook?'

'Caitlin and I went at it together. We bought books and experimented. Nearly poisoned ourselves several times. I haven't done any since. Eat out of tins and Marks & Spencer. It doesn't matter any more. All I have to do is keep alive. I suppose.'

'Might as well take some pleasure as well. Silly not to really.' She leant across the table and touched his arm. Her hand swooped quickly, like a bird, and just grazed the cuff of his shirt and was away again. 'It's not disloyalty to begin to find pleasures again.'

'You don't know what you're talking about.'

'Maybe not. I'm quite sensible though, in spite of all appearances to the contrary.'

'I never said you weren't.'

'I know you didn't. Tell me some more about Caitlin.'

He looked uneasy.

'I don't mean about her death. Nothing like that. The living person – I'd like to know about her.' She smiled at him, a shadow of her mother's smile. 'Please.'

'I have all her paintings at home, stacked round the wall of her studio – well, it's a shed really, down at the bottom of the garden. We put in electricity and running water and I did a bit of insulation. She preferred to work there than in the house. She could ignore the telephone, people coming to the door, me. "I am going to the office," she used to say, and then she'd run out of the kitchen door and down the garden. There was this big window looking out over the sea. Cold north light, like a searchlight. You can't hide anything with a cold north light.'

He looked anxious.

'I hope they're all right – the pictures, not damp or anything. I have neglected them. I haven't even looked at them for ages. I couldn't bear to. I ought to have checked on the roof and things like that. It's quite exposed, just there almost on the edge.' He smiled at her. 'The way you like to be. She liked that too.'

'I'm sure they'll be all right. But you want to take them out of there, hang them on your walls. That's what pictures are for. Are they good? Sorry, I hope that's not a rude question to ask.'

'To be honest, I don't know. I think so, but I don't know. She had been working very hard and was about to have a one-woman show when . . .'

He took an orange from the bowl on the table and dug his thumbnail into it. An aromatic jet shot out of the fruit onto his sleeve.

'There was some stuff in the car with her. That's gone, but the gallery sent the rest back to me for my decision. I haven't made that yet.'

He stripped a curlicue of peel and let it fall onto his plate.

'I was quite pleased that some of her work went with her. I liked the notion that she arrived wherever she was going with baggage, a passport. Just a passing thought. A late night, no sleeping thought. You understand that.'

'I do indeed.'

'People said she was good. I couldn't say. They looked good to me – perhaps a bit obscure. She used to have to explain them to me. I have no background of looking at paintings, only the rubbish you get in churches here. Saints, holy-looking people. And of course the awful things that most people hang on their walls.'

Neatly he broke the orange into segments and made a pattern on his plate. He stared down at them.

'Vitamin C,' he said at last. 'She always used to say that. She made me eat an orange every day. "Don't forget your vitamin C," she would say.' Abruptly he pushed the plate towards Clara. 'You eat it. I don't want it.'

She picked up a piece and put it in her mouth.

'Go on,' she said.

He looked bewildered.

'Tell me more about her.'

'She is escaping. Little by little. I feel every time I mention her name or talk about her in any way that a little bit more of her slips away. Out of my mouth. I am losing her in my breath. Soon, I feel I won't have anything of her left. I will have to look at photographs of her, and maybe I'll even wonder, Is that really Caitlin? Who can that be? Did I know that woman once?'

Clara sighed. 'Eat some orange.'

Obediently he put out a hand and took a segment. He put it into his mouth and chewed; a trickle of juice trailed from the corner of his lips.

'I thought I could keep her locked in my mind. Bright. Quite unchanging.'

'I don't think anyone can do that. I really don't think anyone should want to do such a thing. It's a bit like imprisoning a spirit. 'To the elements be free, and fare thou well . . .' That's what Prospero said to Ariel.'

'Ariel was enslaved.'

'I think you should say the same thing to Caitlin.'

He took another piece of orange and chewed at it angrily.

'What do you know about it? What do you know what I should and shouldn't do with my life? What do you know about love?'

She didn't think there was much point in answering.

Pansy got up from her place by the Aga and clicked her way across the floor; she put her head on Lar's knee and gazed into his face. He scratched at the top of her head with a finger.

'Maybe I don't know much about love,' Clara whispered.

'What we had was special.'

'That's what they all say. Forgive me, I don't want to be cynical about this or hard-hearted, but if you are capable of love at all, then you will find it again. It will not be the same, but it can be equally special. That's a proven fact.'

'I wish to mourn for ever.'

'What a priggish thing to say.'

'It's true.'

'I don't believe you. And what's more, I don't believe that Caitlin would have wanted you to. You make her sound like a woman who liked living.'

He didn't say anything.

'Have a glass of brandy?'

He shook his head.

'Well, I will.'

She got up and went over to the cupboard, took out a squat bottle and a glass and brought them back to the table.

'I will regret this,' she said, as she poured.

'Why do it then?'

'Because I love the feeling of the warm spirit creeping down the back of my throat. Because I know that after one glass I will sleep like a log. Because I would like to feel benign. You don't make me feel benign; maybe the brandy will.'

He laughed. 'You're an odd one. She probably would have liked you.'

She held the glass up towards him.

'Sláinte.'

'Aye. Maybe I'll have a glass after all. Maybe we could both be benign for a while.'

*   *   *

I lie here now thinking about love.

Yes.

The light stirs on the ceiling of my room; branches, twigs, budding leaves, all pattern and re-pattern in the wind. I could, if I wished, pretend that I was lying out of doors, staring up into the trees.

Yes.

Maybe he was right.

Maybe I do know nothing about love. I have perhaps devoured life and people too fast, like a greedy child who eats her ice cream quicker than all the others and then expects them to share their melting cones with her.

'Clara will be all right when she steadies herself,' I once heard Mother say to someone.

'Steady the Buffs,' was an expression my father used and then having used it, he would explain its military connotations.

I don't feel I want to be steady, but I do want to find out about love.

Sleep is snatching at me.

I thought I loved James.

The love words slip in and out of my head.

Joy, longing, excitement, laughter, glory.

Three months.

Steady the Buffs.

I thought we were growing together, knitting and knotting our senses and our thoughts. Love was happening – I thought. I knew that I had only fiddled at love before. The slate was wiped clean by James. I had no past, no present, no future, except with him. I was so sure of that.

St . . . ea . . . dy the Buffs!

The branches on the ceiling drift lower and lower. If I lift my hand I will be able to touch them. If I lift my head from the pillow they will tangle in my hair.

What is love? 'tis not hereafter;
Present mirth hath present laughter;
What's to come is still unsure.

Clara will be all right when she . . .

Gioir.

I used to see his face when I closed my eyes. I used to feel his hand on my skin when I was alone. I used to hear his voice in my dreams.

I still feel the weight of his expensive gold watch clasped around my wrist. I sometimes wonder why I didn't smash it into bits with a hammer and send him the pieces in a Jiffy bag, preferably without stamps on it, so that he would have had to pay to spill the shards of glass and metal out onto his breakfast table.

The branches settle gently on my face like soft fingers. I will sleep.

☆ ☆ ☆

Lar, on the other hand, did not sleep.

The brandy throbbed in his head, made his heart race, did, in fact, all the things that he had known it would do.

He wondered why he had not told Clara the truth.

He wondered why he had told her mother.

Clara, he felt would nag on and on at him, prying into his privacies, giving him undoubtedly, her strident views on the North, terrorists, Unionists, Republicans, history, religion and all the rest of that stuff that people went on and on and on about. People who didn't know, people who didn't care, people who didn't hurt. How dare she suggest that Caitlin would have wanted him to make a new life, to be content with shadowy memories, to become in some way normal once more. Intolerable notion. Intolerable woman.

He groaned.

Pansy on the floor at the foot of the bed gave a little whimper. He saw his mother standing by the clock in the hall, wearing grey; she stretched out a hand towards him. He turned over and dug his face into the pillow. The image fractured into tears.

*   *   *

The telephone is ringing.

Where am I?

I always laugh when that question comes into my mind.

Dublin or New York?

My life seems to be punctuated by the ringing of the telephone.

That is not a New York bell that rings.

I grope.

Where the hell is the bloody machine anyway? I am going to have to open my eyes.

I should never have had that brandy.

Now I know where I am.

Now I know who is ringing.

As I scoop up the receiver I struggle to put one foot on the floor.

'Did I wake you?'

'I am up.' I am very uncomfortable, one foot on the floor, the

other tangled in the bedclothes. Outside the window the sun is
sending red glory up into the sky.

'I met that man yesterday afternoon.'

'He told me.'

'Laurence.'

'Yes. So?'

'I hate that "so?" It's so aggressive.'

I think of saying it again, but decide against it.

'Current parlance,' I say instead.

'How was your dinner?'

'Great. He's quite a cook.'

'He was looking for a chicken.'

'He found one.'

I can hear the wheels in her mind turning. I am not going to
help her out. I remain silent. I even try not to breathe; perhaps
she will forget that I am here and go and make some jam.

'Clara.'

'Yes?'

'I thought maybe you'd dropped off to sleep again.'

'I am up, Mother.'

'I think you should dispatch him back to wherever it is he
comes from. Somewhere near Ballycastle, I think he said. Your
father and I went to the Old Lammas Fair once. I didn't think
much of it. A lot of tinkers. As far as I can remember, it rained.'

'Dispatch sounds like bringing him down to the post office
and putting a stamp on him.'

'You know what I mean. It would be the sensible thing to do.'

'When have you ever known me to be sensible?'

'I live in hope, dear. That's all I rang to say. I have given it a

lot of thought. I slept quite restlessly last night; I presume it
was because of Laurence.'

'What nonsense.'

'When I get worried I find it difficult to sleep.'

'That's a problem for the doctor, not for me. I don't need you
to worry about me, Mother. I can do my own worrying. And
there's no point in worrying about Lar, either. He's a passing
stranger. He'll go when it pleases him and neither of us will see
him again.'

'I hope it will be soon. It's not that I dislike him. I just think
he should go home.'

'And I think I must go and sit down at my writing machine.'

'I have just made a batch of brown bread. Would you like me
to bring you round a couple of loaves?'

'No, thanks.'

'You could put them in the deep freeze.'

'My deep freeze is bursting with loaves of brown bread.'

Silence.

'Thank you all the same.'

A small sigh.

'I must go, Mother.'

'I'll ring you later, when you're up.'

'I am up!'

End of call.

Nothing for it but to get to work.

Broadening the Horizons

The Gingerbread Woman

(continued)

'I think we should broaden our horizons a bit,' I told him.

He sat up and swung his legs over the side of the bed. He stretched out his golden arms in front of him and clicked his wrists, a habit of his that always made me feel a little sick, just for a moment, nothing important enough to mention to him.

'Tired of me?' he asked.

'Darling!'

'Sounds like it to me. What does that mean, broadening horizons?' He got up and walked towards the bathroom. He was golden all over, like a piece made by Cellini, smooth and perfect. I had never cared before, now I was overjoyed by just the sight of him.

'I just thought that perhaps we might find out a little more about each other. Go places, meet each other's friends, check out our mutual likes and dislikes.' I was beginning to sound American, I thought.

He went into the bathroom without speaking and turned on the shower. The smell of steam and shower gel floated into the room.

'I mean to say,' I called out, 'there *is* a world out there.'

I didn't know if he could hear me, or even if he wanted to hear me. Maybe this is a crisis in our relationship, I thought. It would be interesting to see how we worked it through.

Eventually he came out of the bathroom, a towel tied around

his waist, his heavy gold watch held in his left hand. He sat down on the bed beside me and touched my hair, then my cheek, the side of my neck. I remember the feel of those touches so well. Then he picked up my left hand and clasped the gold watch bracelet round my wrist. He kissed my hand.

'I have been so selfish.' He murmured the words onto the back of my hand. His eyes were shut and I think I imagined tears which quivered at the side of his closed lids.

'What's this?'

'It's for you. I notice that you have no watch. Without a watch, my darling, you might be late for your own funeral.'

'You can't give me that. It looks terribly precious.'

He laughed, opened his eyes and threw back his head. 'It *is* terribly precious. The first present from me to you. You are terribly precious.'

'I won't argue with that.'

'Come on, lazybones. Stir yourself. Put some clothes on and we'll take a walk.'

'What about dinner?'

'What about it? Dinner can wait.'

He was dressing as he spoke. Inch by inch the golden skin was being covered with silk and fine cotton, and then soft shaved wool. His clothes were almost as seductive as he was. He looked at me and smiled.

'Up, up,' he said.

'I don't want to go and walk. At least not now. Not till I've had my dinner. I'm starving. I had no lunch.'

He continued to smile.

'Whatever you say.'

'We'll give it a miss tonight. Anyway, that's not quite the point.' I got up and put on my dressing-gown. 'I just feel it's time for a bit of normality to happen.'

He was putting on his tie, turning his head from side to side as he always did as he centred the knot.

'Will we be able to survive normality?' I demanded.

He laughed.

'Foolish woman. Of course we will. We can survive anything.'

'I wonder. I'd just like to test out normality. I don't want to do anything dangerous.'

Gently he pushed me through the door and into the other room. The table was laid, the candles already lit. He settled me into a chair and handed me a plate.

'Eat,' he ordered. He pulled his own chair close to mine and began to heap food onto his plate.

'I didn't have any lunch either. Look, honey, you have to trust me on this one. I have this major problem with my mother. Major, major.'

He poured us each some wine and took a long slug. 'As I think I tried to explain, obviously not very well, but it depresses the hell out of me to talk much about the scene, she depended so heavily on my dad and now she's transferred that dependence to me. And I'm scared – really scared. She's always been a bitch out of hell about any ladies I have had in my life. In fact, she most effectively got rid of them all, one by one.' He pointed the two fingers of his right hand at me. 'Poum, poum, poum.'

I laughed.

'No laughing matter. Now I have found you, I don't want you to be vaporised. I want you in my life like I've never wanted anyone else. So we have to play it cool, Clara.'

He stroked my arm with his finger.

'You see, though she can be awful on one level, she's also very fragile, and in spite of all the things she perpetrates on me, I love her.'

I loved the tenderness in his voice.

'Anything you say,' I muttered.

'You understand?'

'I suppose I do. Well, to be quite honest, no I don't, but I'm trying very hard.' I shovelled a lot of food into my mouth and chewed vigorously. 'You know I'm only here until July.'

He looked startled.

'Clara . . .'

'About the middle of July at the latest. My job will be over and Jodie will be wanting her flat back. My visa runs out then and I will have to start looking for another job. Where will I go next?'

I think he thought I was joking.

'Shanghai?' he suggested. 'Katmandu? Samarkand? I will come with you. I will be your bodyguard, your personal assistant, your jack of all trades.'

'Don't forget to bring your mother.' My voice must have sounded sarcastic, for he blushed. 'Sorry,' I said, then I wondered why I had apologised. After all, I was the one who had been talking about reality. It was about time that we began to recognise that neither of us was as totally charming as we appeared.

'I'm not joking,' I said. 'Come in, Clara Barry, your time is up.'

He looked puzzled. I didn't bother to explain.

'It never occurred to me that you might have to leave.'

'We haven't had that sort of conversation.'

'No.'

He pushed his plate away, he reached across the table and took my hands in his. He held them tight; this was no caress, they were prisoners.

'Listen to me, Clara.' He paused, as if he didn't know what to say next. 'Listen. I can't collect my thoughts on this. All I know is that I don't want you to go. I *can't* let you go. I have to take my mother down to Connecticut tomorrow. I'll be away a week, but I promise you I'm going to do a lot of thinking. If things go smoothly with her I'll talk to her about you. Lay down some tracks. I see by your face that you think I'm nuts, but you'll have to trust me on this one. Maybe if I can persuade her to stay in the country, we can get more time together, go away together. Maybe I could take a vacation in Ireland with you. Meet your folks. All sorts of maybes.'

'All sorts.'

'Let's drink to that.'

He let go of my hands and picked up his glass.

'To our future.'

'To our future.'

*   *   *

I am despising myself as I write.

I have always despised stupidity in others so, as is the way of the world I have been hoisted with my own petard – whatever that may mean. We trot out these phrases day after day without inspecting them in any way; our mothers and fathers said them, so it is OK for us to carry on. Anyway, that particular phrase makes me feel that I am hanging by one leg from a lamp-post somewhere for all to see and comment on. Of course, if you look at it from another angle, the world would be a poor place if none of us was prepared to make fools of ourselves. I will take the dog for a walk and clear my head. It is time to stop when such tiresome thoughts clog up the brain.

I turn on the bath taps and drip a lot of healing and soothing oils into the swirling water.

I wonder why Mother has taken against poor Lar in the way she has? He seems more pathetic than dangerous to me. Maybe he spun her some romantic yarn about being on the run, wanted by police or terrorists or perhaps even both. She wouldn't like that at all. Then I decide that if that was what he had said, she'd have packed him off there and then, not even giving him time to come back and collect his clothes and the dog.

The bath is definitely a good place to be; a safe place, a calm place, a healing place . . . as long as you don't think about Charlotte Corday — but then, of course, she operated under rather different circumstances. It is unlikely that Lar will creep in and cut my throat.

Branches rustle on the small window. I must get out one sunny day and do some pruning, otherwise when the summer comes the sun won't penetrate the leaves of clematis and jasmine and this room will be dark.

Lather runs from my arms, slithers down into the water. The thrum of strict rhythm, a sudden melody, then the sax, oh my God what an instrument. How did they ever live before the sax was invented?

Piano.

Down, slipping down. This is what having a bath is all about, I push myself further and further down into the embracing water.

Booodeedoooo.

Oooh, how . . .

Piano melody once more

Runs. Trills. Water smoothing. Saxoooophone.

Yes. Oh yes.

Like this I feel so . . .

Warm, so glowing warm.

Lovely?

I feel I can once more be lovely.

Yes.

Maybe I will be . . . Yes.

Glow.

Saxo . . . glow. Then drums. Soft, vibrating through the water . . . oooh lovely. I will rise now, break through the water with the drums.

Drums a bit loud there. Shake the water from out of the ears. Surface. Steam, shining skin, soapy bubbles. Out here maybe it will be cold.

Drums, drums. Oh heck!

'For heaven's sake Clara, you're wanted on the telephone.'

Heck.

'Clara.' He has opened the bathroom door, the better to be heard, I presume, and is standing discreetly outside it.

'Come in why don't you and join the sing-song. I'm singing in the bath.'

'Telephone.' His voice is quiet but exasperated. 'If it's Mother tell her no. Tell her I've had my ration for this morning. Tell her

I'm hard at work and must on no account be . . .'

'It's not your mother. It's a man called Ivan. He says he's your doctor.'

For a moment I consider heaving myself out of the bath, wrapping a towel round myself and dripping to the phone. Idiotic thought.

'Tell him no.'

'No, what?'

'Just no. Clara says no. Quite simple.'

He sighs. I hear his feet moving along the passage.

'Shut the door!' I yell. Then I tell myself that I must not be hard on this poor bereaved man. 'Please!'

I hear his feet once more and the door closes quietly. But it's too late now. The bath magic is gone. I can no longer hear the sax or piano. I can no longer rustle up the harsh and magic voice of Billie Holiday. I sigh now in my turn and pull out the plug with my toes.

*　*　*

'Clara says no.' He repeated her words obediently, he presuming that whoever it was at the other end of the line would accept them without investigation.

'God, but she's a cheeky child. Is that all she said?'

'She's in the bath.'

'Ah well, that explains everything. Who are you anyway?'

Lar wondered for a moment who he was, and what the hell he was doing there answering the telephone for a nutcase.

'I . . .'

'Sorry, rude question. I take it back. You're from the North,

I can hear that in your voice. Staying for long?'

'I don't . . .'

'Sorry, another inappropriate question. It's because I'm a doctor. My head is full of inappropriate questions. Keep having to ask them to my patients. Tell Clara I'll give her another ring sometime. Cheers.'

He was gone. Lar put down the telephone.

'Cheers,' he said to no one.

He picked up the dog's lead and snapped it onto her collar.

'I'm not hanging around here till she gets out of her bath,' he muttered to Pansy, who wagged her tail, pleased to be addressed.

They left the house and headed up to the top of the hill and then turned down a winding road that led towards the sea. The air was still, waiting he felt for the leaves to burst open or for some rare and important person to pass by, stepping lightly across the tended gardens, over the damp morning grass, leaving no trace behind, displacing only air. He felt that presence strongly. He felt as if he and the dog were the only other moving beings. He could hear no sounds but the dog's panting breath as she strained at her lead, anxious to get to wherever they were going, and the scuff of his own feet on the narrow footpath. I am perhaps dead, he thought. At that moment when I put down the telephone, I died and this is the landscape I must walk through to reach eternity, or maybe Caitlin.

He began to run, the dog loping beside him. They turned a corner, went under a railway bridge and then swinging to the left, emerged into a car park just above a long stony beach. He stepped over a low stone wall and bent to slip off Pansy's lead.

As he stood up again he heard the rattling of the sea and the mournful mew of a gull that was circling overhead. The dog ran eagerly towards the sea, barking at the twisting waves, the way she always did at home.

A train rattled along the tracks behind him.

He walked slowly towards the rocks that were heaped between the railway and the sea.

What would happen to Pansy if I were to walk out into that sea? he wondered. So far from home. Would she find her way back to Clara's house, or would she just run desperately up and down this long beach, searching for me and whining, running eagerly up to lone walkers and then, discouraged, slinking away again? Would she mourn me until she died of desperation? He rather liked that thought.

'Damn,' he said. 'What a sentimental fool I am.'

He heard Caitlin laugh behind him and turned quickly to catch a glimpse of her.

'I know you're here,' he said to the air.

He sat down on a damp rock and put his head in his hands.

The wind touched his hair like gentle fingers, smoothed at his forehead, stroked the backs of his hands.

He heard the steps walk past him towards the sea, a little crunch, a little shuffle, a stone or two kicked sideways. Light steps. He looked up and saw no one.

'Caitlin.'

About a hundred yards away Pansy was shaking the life out of some seaweed that she had pulled up the beach from the water's edge. She shook it and growled and threw it in the air and yapped and shook it again.

Another train passed behind him, carrying people to their work in the city.

He heard the steps again, scuffing up from the sea.

'Caitlin.'

The wind became her soft breath.

'I don't know why you're playing games with me.'

She touched his hair and his face. Maybe she even kissed him, brushing her lips across his cheek. He stretched out his arms but only embraced emptiness.

'I want to see you.'

She was going. He felt her moving away. Her hand touched his shoulder for the last time, her fingers held for a moment his wrist. The wind seemed to whisper. He strained his head forward to hear the words. It wasn't the wind, it was the waves creeping and turning, sighing and singing.

'*To the elements be free, and fare thou well.*'

Damn that Clara woman, her words following him to the beach, whispering with the waves, teasing him. It was Caitlin's voice he needed to hear.

He jumped to his feet, startled by the sound of running footsteps. A man ran past him, flicked a smile in his direction and then pounded straight without pause into the sea, throwing himself forward and swimming out strongly, heading apparently for the horizon.

Pansy abandoned the seaweed and came trotting back to Lar. They both stood and watched the swimmer. After about two minutes he turned and swam back to the shore. He pelted up the beach, past Lar and the dog.

'It's great,' he panted. 'You should try it.'

✻　✻　✻

The smell of frying bacon hit him when he came in the door. She was singing again — caterwauling, you might call it.

'Der Frühling will Kommen . . .'

He was hungry, even after that pile of dinner he'd eaten last night.

'Der Frühling meine Freud.'

Awful scrapy scratchy voice, he thought.

Pansy barged past him and into the kitchen.

The singing stopped.

'Hi,' she called out. 'You're just in time.'

She bent down and patted Pansy.

'Good morning, dog. I had decided to take her for a run and then when I discovered that you'd already left, I thought I'd cook us a huge breakfast instead. Where did you go?'

'Down to the sea. Pansy likes the sea.'

He paused for a moment and wondered whether to tell her about what had happened on the beach. Better not, he thought. Better not tell anyone that sort of thing. Anyway, maybe nothing had happened; just a man swam and ran and spoke to him.

'The sea air cleared my head. Made me hungry.'

'Good. Sit down.'

'We seem to spend our lives eating.'

She laughed.

'Punctuation marks. Commas, full stops, even semicolons. Think about it. This meal is a semicolon; your coffee with my mother yesterday a comma.'

He shook his head.

'No,' he said. 'I think that was more like the end of a paragraph.'

'Full stop, new line?'

'Something like that.'

The food was good. He was ravenous. He ate greedily, heaping his plate with fried bread and bursting fat sausages, tomatoes and bacon. He slathered toast with butter and marmalade and drank umpteen cups of tea. He sat back at last with a huge sigh.

'Wow,' she said. Then they both began to laugh. He held his hands out to her across the table and they laughed and laughed, clutching at each other's fingers as if to stop themselves falling on the floor. As suddenly as they had started, they stopped and stared at each other, bewildered.

'I'm not allowed to laugh,' she said when she got her breath back.

'What was all that about?'

'I don't know.'

'Weird,' she said.

Gently she disentangled her fingers from his.

'I haven't done that since I was a child, laughed myself almost sick for no reason.'

'I hope it hasn't opened up your wound.'

'I shouldn't think so. Joggled everything around inside me quite a bit. But that's no harm.'

She leant forward and touched his face.

'Are you all right?'

'May I use your telephone? I think I'll give my parents a bell, if I may. I won't talk for long.'

'You can talk as long as you bloody well like. Use the phone by my bed.'

'Thanks.'

He went into her room and sat cautiously on the unmade bed. She didn't use a duvet, he noticed. He'd have thought she'd be a bit more up to date than fiddling around with sheets and blankets. A lot of pillows were heaped at the head of the bed. He bent and let his head droop into the hollow where her head had lain.

His mother had always said that sleeping with more than one pillow was bad for you – bad for the spine, and probably for the soul, he thought; too much comfort definitely leading to a decline in moral standards. He wanted to laugh again, lie here on Clara's bed and yell with laughter, make the ornaments on her mantelpiece rattle, shake the pictures off their hooks, and set the curtains swinging.

'Not,' he said aloud, 'that I have anything to laugh about.' He got up from the bed and walked back into the kitchen. She was sitting where he had left her. She looked round as he came into the room.

'That was quick,' she said.

'I haven't done it yet.'

'Cold feet?'

'Something like that.'

'I should ring them if I were you. You're going to have to do it sometime, no point in putting it off and off. Unless . . .'

'Unless what?'

'Unless you don't mean to ring them at all. Just disappear out of their lives. Phhhttt. You don't seem to be that sort of man to me. So ring them sooner rather than later.'

'You know nothing about what goes on in my head.'

'That's true. But you don't seem to me to be cruel.'

He considered the word with care. He didn't like it.

'I am not cruel.'

'Have another cup of tea?'

He shook his head.

'Coffee?'

'For heaven's sake,' he said in exasperation.

'Well, at least tell me what all this is about. I can't give you advice if—'

'I never asked you for advice. I don't need advice. I can advise myself.'

She raised her eyebrows but said nothing.

'The trouble with women is that they either offer you tea or advice.'

'Or both,' she said.

'Are we joking here? I thought we were being serious. Why do you have to joke?'

'It wasn't meant as a joke, merely a rather banal reflection on myself. Do sit down. I hate people standing over me.' She sipped her tea and watched him as he walked round the table and sat down.

'Anyway,' she said after a long silence, 'the tea's cold. You wouldn't have got much joy from it.'

'I don't really understand why you would suggest that I am cruel.'

'Sorry. Definitely the wrong word. I am sorry. I think I

probably meant thoughtless. Careless of other people's feelings.'

'I don't know why you're saying these things to me.'

'You asked me to.'

'I did not.'

'Maybe not in so many words.'

'Definitely not in any words at all.'

She sighed.

'I'm sorry. I didn't want to upset you. I just thought you needed help.'

'Help?'

'Yes.'

'Everyone wants to help me. That's why I had to get away. I want to be left alone.'

'You and Greta Garbo.'

He slammed his hands down on the table.

'Don't bloody do that!'

She stood up.

'I'm going to get dressed now. I hate being shouted at. You people from up there are so prickly, it's no wonder you can't get along with anyone else, let alone yourselves.'

'Stupid.'

'Yes. Stupid.'

She turned and walked out of the room.

He began to clear the table, piling the plates up beside the sink, scraping the remains of bacon rinds, crusts and crumbs into the bin, just as Caitlin had taught him to do. His mother had always excused him from such chores. 'Laurence is tired. Laurence has his homework to do. Go you on away, Laurence. I can manage, I'm sure you've better things to do.'

Always, Mum, always.

He turned on the tap and squirted some washing-up liquid into the basin. That woman was singing again in her bedroom; if you could call it singing. Big if!

He wondered what Caitlin had really meant on the beach.

Goodbye?

Get on.

That would be quite like her.

Get on.

Sometimes when he had exasperated her she would say that. 'Oh Lar, get on,' or even, 'Do let me get on, Lar.'

Fare thou well. She needed rid of him. Was that it?

He heard her voice quite clearly: '*Dead. We are a long time dead, Lar. Oh Lar, for heaven's sake get on.*'

For some reason his right foot was wet. He looked down and saw that hot water and bubbles were streaming out over the top of the sink and cascading onto the floor, soaking his right foot.

'Bugger.'

He turned off the tap and plunged his hand and part of his arm into the hot water, searching for the plug.

'Bugger, bugger.'

'*Long time dead.*'

He found it and pulled. His hand was almost cooked and the sleeve of his jersey soaking.

'*Do get on, Lar, and give me a bit of peace.*'

The water level in the basin was sinking. His hand was throbbing. The bubbles made a quiet sighing sound.

'What in the name of God are you doing?'

Clara was standing in the doorway.

'Washing up. But . . .'

'You've had a little mishap.'

'I . . . Yes. I was thinking. I'm . . .'

'Well, clear up all that water. Don't just stand there. Your trousers will dry quick enough in front of the Aga and I do have a dish-washer in case you hadn't noticed. All mod cons in this house. Why plunge your hands in and out of hot water if you don't have to?'

'I'm sorry.'

'That's OK, I'm sorry I flew off the handle. You'll find cloths in the cupboard under the sink and a mop outside the back door. Are you all right? You look rotten.' She took a step into the room. 'Is there anything I can do?'

He looked at her in silence, almost as if he didn't know who she was. Then he said, 'It's all over.'

She walked to the table and pulled out a chair. 'Sit down. Here, take off those trousers first.'

'They're all right.'

'Just take them off and don't be silly. Ten minutes will see them dry.'

He bent down and pulled off his shoes and then struggled out of his trousers. She held out her hand and he gave them to her. She tucked them neatly over the bar along the front of the Aga. He was still standing there looking absurd when she turned round. She pointed to the chair and he sat down.

'What's all over?'

She sat beside him and touched him gently on the shoulder. He shook his head.

They both waited unmoving to see who would speak next.

Eventually Lar did.

'I'm really not crazy.'

'I never thought you were.'

'Thanks.'

'What is all over?'

'I thought she would want me to . . .'

Oh God, thought Clara, how I hate long meaningful pauses.

'. . . mourn for ever.'

'No one can do that. No one can be expected to do that. Remember with joy is a good thing to do, but then get on.'

'That's what she said — "get on".'

'Who?'

'Caitlin.'

He spoke the name so quietly that she thought she had heard him wrong.

'Who?'

'Caitlin.'

'But . . . when did she say that?'

'This morning, on the beach. She spoke. She was there. She touched me. She spoke.'

Clara scratched at her chin with a finger and stared past him out of the window.

'You met Caitlin on the beach this morning?'

'Well, not quite met, but she was there. She spoke to me.'

Clara sighed.

'Clara . . .'

'What did she say?'

' "To the elements be free, and fare thou well" .'

'But,' she said, remembering their conversation, then: 'Well, that's OK then, isn't it? I thought you were going to come out with some long and soulful spiel. A sort of ghostlike diatribe. But that is good sensible stuff.' She smiled at him. 'I'd pay attention to that if I were you.'

The doorbell rang.

Pansy lifted her head and looked first at Lar and then at Clara.

'The bell,' said Lar.

She nodded and got up.

Pansy stretched her back out to its full length and opened and closed her front paws; she then sat up and looked expectantly towards the door.

It was the doctor on the doorstep.

'Heavens,' said Clara. 'I thought you were in Oughterard.'

'I came home.'

'But you rang about an hour ago. I presumed you were calling from there.'

'I was at home. May I come in?'

'Why not?'

She stood aside and he walked past her and down the passage into the kitchen.

Lar was struggling to get into his trousers. Pansy thumped her tail on the floor once or twice and then lay down and closed her eyes.

'What a nice domestic scene,' said the doctor.

'I didn't ask for a house call.'

'I'm on holiday. How about a cup of coffee? How do you do? I think we've spoken on the telephone.'

He held his hand out towards Lar.

'This is Lar. Laurence McGrane. Lar, my doctor.'

Lar finished shoving his shirt into the top of his trousers and shook the man's hand. The right trouser leg was still sopping wet. The doctor's hand was cool and soft – just, he thought, as a medical man's hands should be.

'Yes,' he said. 'Hello there. Yes, well, I was just drying my trousers.'

Clara moved the kettle onto the hotplate. 'Were the fish not biting?'

He pulled out a chair and sat down at the table. 'Your mother rang me.'

'Mother? Is she not well? I had supper with her the day before yesterday and she seemed OK.'

'She's fine. She just thought I ought to come home. So I did. I pay a lot of heed to what your mother says to me. Mind if I smoke?'

'Be my guest.'

She turned away and taking the coffee-pot down from the shelf began to spoon coffee into it. The doctor offered his cigarette packet to Lar.

'Smoke?'

'No, thanks.'

'Sensible man. I only do when off duty. Even that's foolish.' He took a lighter from his pocket and lit his cigarette. He inhaled deeply and then let the smoke slowly out through his nose. Clara picked up the kettle and poured boiling water onto the coffee. Lar wondered what was going on. Pansy smiled in her sleep.

'So what did Mother have on her mind?' The doctor gave a

little laugh. 'She seemed to think that you weren't looking after yourself very well.' He held his hand up to stop her speaking. 'I told her I'd seen you the other day and that you looked all right to me, but she seemed concerned, so . . .' He took another deep pull on his cigarette. 'You know how she is. The weather wasn't great for fishing anyway. I missed Dublin. My sister-in-law is a lovely woman but there's little calm around her household. I longed for silence. Am I doing OK?'

'No. I really object to being treated like this. My mother is intolerable. You know as well as I do, how intolerable she is. You should pay no attention to her.' She pushed the plunger down in the coffee-pot.

'Too soon,' the doctor said. 'You should let it brew for five minutes.'

'Do not tell me what to do in my own kitchen.'

She poured some coffee into a mug and pushed it across the table towards him. He ignored it.

'Coffee, Lar?'

'Perhaps I should . . . ah . . .'

She poured some more coffee and handed it to him.

'Sit down and drink it. Don't go.'

'I . . .' He looked uneasily towards the door.

'Oh, for heaven's sake sit down and pay no attention to him.'

'Yes, do please sit down,' said the doctor pleasantly. 'Do what she says. It's easier in the long run.'

Lar sat down and took a sip from his mug. It was pretty disgusting. They sat in silence for a long time. The doctor yawned. He picked up his mug of coffee and inspected it.

'As I thought. Undrinkable.'

'Why don't you just go home?'

'This is a house call. I'm drawing it out as long as I can and then my secretary will be able to send you a huge bill.'

'Why don't you go and make a house call with Mother?'

'Your mother has nothing wrong with her.'

'She will have after I've dealt with her.'

'Come, come, Clara. You're being a bit unfair. She just has your best interests at heart. I'll have to dilute this poison with milk.'

'It's in the fridge.' She didn't move to get it and neither did he.

Lar got up and went over to the fridge. He opened the door and took out a carton of milk. Behind him he heard Clara's voice sink to an angry whisper.

'Just fuck off, Doctor.'

The doctor didn't reply.

Lar put the carton on the table and sat down again. He hated other people's rows. In fact, he hated all rows. Caitlin had found it to be one of the unsatisfactory things about him, his facility for escaping when even a small argument was in the offing. *'You disappear, become invisible. It's like talking to a shadow on the wall. You don't seem to realise that people need a good fight sometimes.'*

He remembered, they had been standing by their bedroom window and the sea below and the sky had been for a brief few minutes one and the same colour, each element disturbed either by racing white waves or tiny clouds that seemed to have taken on the rhythm of the waves below them.

'Look. We are submerged,' he had said, and he remembered her laughing at his inattention.

'How long are you planning on staying?'

Lar realised that the doctor was talking to him.

'Ah, sorry. Term starts next week.' He avoided answering the question.

'You're a teacher?'

'Yes. Mathematics.'

'Are you going to go back?'

Lar hesitated.

'I think so,' he said at last. He then realised that Clara was no longer there; at some moment as he had lingered in the past, she must have left the room.

'Where's Clara?'

'She was about to hit me, but decided to leave the room instead. I actually think she may be in the garden. Her mother told me your very tragic story.'

'Oh yes.'

'Is there anything I can do to help you?'

'I shouldn't think so. Thanks.'

'Sometimes people can help, you know.'

'I do not need help. I have told everyone that. They're all so full of suggestions, goodwill, love. I just want to be allowed to . . . hate the world in peace.'

'Fair enough,' said the doctor. 'That's OK by me. I just don't want you messing up Clara's life.'

'How could I do that? I hardly know the woman. She has been kind to me, yes. Given me and the dog a bit of comfort. Why would I mess up her life? She doesn't think I'm mad although almost everyone else does. I'd have thought that as a doctor you would understand. You all talk about her as being

post-operative . . . what the hell do you think I am? I've had half
my life, my being hacked off, without a bloody anaesthetic. I
live in constant raging pain.'

Laurence leant his elbows on the table and put his head in his
hands. 'There have been times when I haven't wanted to go on
living. There have been times when I have wanted to kill someone.
You know, I have this picture of this man running over the hill.
I know in my head exactly what he looks like and I swear to you,
Doctor, that if I were to meet him in the street I would kill him.'

He looked up at the other man.

'I bet you'd like to lock me up.'

The doctor shook his head.

'We could do that, all right. Fill you with drugs – all that
sort of thing. But people who don't want to mend don't mend.
I expect you've listened to a lot of words over the last couple of
years.'

'Yes.'

'I won't add to them then.'

'Thanks.'

A shaft of light through the window all of a sudden gilded
half the room. The doctor sat, unaware, the cigarette in his
hand; he looked newly lacquered, Lar thought, all golden but a
bit forlorn.

'Quick.' It was Clara calling from the garden. 'Oh, do come
quickly.'

The two men and Pansy jumped to their feet and ran outside.
Clara was standing by the gate.

The sun had bathed the garden and street in a fierce golden
light. The sky was mostly black with clouds, but the low sun

shone straight down the street through the trees like a golden spotlight. Everything it touched seemed magnified and quite still. Clara held out her golden hands towards the men. They stood by the gate as still as the trees and the little house and the golden mess of last year's unkempt flowerbeds.

'We are transformed,' whispered Clara. 'We have become angels.' The sun was so dazzling that she had to close her eyes. A little wind rustled in the hedge and like a wolf the black clouds consumed the sun and everything was grey once more.

Clara opened her eyes. The three of them stood there holding hands and suddenly looking rather foolish.

'Well, I'm sorry. That was a bit daft, but I thought it was something amazing. Something weird. I needed somebody else to see it too.'

'It's going to rain,' said Lar, removing his hand from hers.

The doctor stared down the road towards the distant grey hills, his face quite weary now. He must be into his fifties, thought Lar; he looks like he needs a rest, or maybe just silence as he said himself, quite a lot of silence. A fat drop fell on the side of his face.

'No, you're not daft,' said the doctor. 'It was strange surely.'

'Do you think the whole city was like that? Spotlit? Under someone's microscope for a minute or two?'

'No, no. The trees on the other side of the road were black. It was just us. God had us for a moment in His eye. Just us.'

'Is that a good thing or a bad thing? What do you think, Lar? You're probably the only one here who believes in God.'

'I think we're going to get soaking wet. Yet again. I'll have to take off my trousers and dry them by your stove. Again, again.'

The drops were coming faster now, exploding as they landed on his face and arms. He turned and hurried along the path and into the house.

She looked at the doctor.

'You're tired.'

He nodded.

'Come on back into the house and I'll make you a proper cup of coffee. I feel amazingly light-hearted. Almost well again. I'll soon be able to run away from my mother once more.'

Meanwhile . . . back in New York

The Gingerbread Woman

(continued)

I can hear their soft voices drifting from the kitchen. Sometimes a little silence and then the murmur starts again. The doctor seems quite determined not to go; maybe when I set off on my next voyage he and Lar will set up house here together. Why do I constantly have such facetious thoughts clogging up my mind? Perhaps this is the reason why I have never become a highly regarded novelist or a major academic, or at any rate some person of substance.

Is humorous self-deprecation a symptom of that middle-class malaise called complacency? What am I doing tapping such nonsense into the seemingly insatiable maw of this miraculous machine? Passing time? And the machine answers sleepily.

ccrrrm.

Its notes are almost musical.

pllling . . . save now or cancel . . . crrrm.

If only I could so easily cancel the last year of my life.

ttt ttt ttt clllm. You may lose material if you continue.

Let's not lose anything.

Let us see what my story looks like after it has been recollected in a certain degree of tranquillity.

James went away for a week.

To me it seemed like a month. We . . . eell not quite true, just seven endless dragging days. I had never been to Connecticut, so I had no notion of the landscape. I was sure that there were trees, at that moment bursting into leaf, early rhododendrons and camellias, perhaps a stream somewhere close, with willows by the bank. Small rolling hills, perhaps. I thought of all these elements of landscape, but I couldn't put them together in my head. So I envisioned him walking in emptiness, semi-dark, alone. Longing for me.

Was his mother dark or fair?

I was sure she wouldn't be grey.

Did she have long fingers, ring-heavy, with which she would brush the sleeve of his cashmere jacket, or touch his cheekbone, just below his right eye? Even the thought of that intimate gesture took my breath away for a moment.

Of course I went to work and out to eat with friends and to the cinema and my life rolled along as it always had done before I had met James Cavan.

My fridge became empty once more.

I couldn't sleep, expecting every moment his call. I imagined him escaping in the car down to the local mall and putting through calls to me from the drugstore or gas station; but he never did. Or slipping out of bed in the early hours of the morning, and creeping to the telephone, whispering my name, delighting in his idiotic bravery, but he never did that either.

He called me on Tuesday. I was eating a yogurt in my office and looking over my notes on *The Last September* when the phone went.

'Hello. Clara Barry.'

There was a long silence and I thought that someone had dialled a wrong number. I was just about to put down the phone when he spoke.

'How formal you are, Clara Barry.'

'I thought you were never coming back again.'

'Where's faith?'

'Who's she?'

'I've missed you so much, darling.'

Try harder, I thought.

'Did you miss me?'

'Of course.'

'Are you working?'

'Yes.'

'I'll go then. I can say all the things I want to say this evening.'

'I'm going to the cinema this evening.'

'You're kidding.'

'I hung around all day yesterday waiting for you to call. I was free last night. I'm always free on Mondays. Mondays, Wednesdays, Thursdays.'

'Cancel it.'

'James . . .'

'I'll see you at seven-thirty.'

He put down the phone.

I put down my yogurt and went in next door to Sophie. She was doing stretching exercises, standing by the window, arms up above her head, bending slowly from side to side.

I stood and watched. She would notice me in her own good time. She let her head roll around, chest, side, back, side. I could hear the rustling and crackling of nodules and whatever else was in there, from where I stood, like old ball-bearings grinding together.

'Hi,' she said at last. She stood up straight, balancing her fingertips on her desk and trying to focus her eyes on me.

'Hi. Sorry to interrupt.'

'I'm in such bad shape. Stiff as a board. I'll have to get in some classes before the vacation strikes. What can I do for you?'

'I can't make it tonight. I'm sorry.'

She looked at me without speaking.

'Something's cropped up.'

'Yeah,' she said at last. 'That guy has cropped up. They always told me the Irish were fools. Now I know it's true.'

She raised her hands from the desk and began to click her fingers.

She held her arms out towards me. Click, click.

'Little Irish puppy dog comes running.'

'You're being a bit rough. I'm just stepping out of a group visit to the cinema.'

Click. Click.

'What has he got that we haven't got?'

'Do you really want me to tell you?'

Click. Click.

'Nah. Forget it. He's obviously quite irresistible. I suppose we won't see you till the end of term now. Is that the way it'll be? At least this time we'll know it wasn't something one of us said.' Click.

'Apologise to the others, will you?' I turned to leave.

'Remember what happened to Little Red Riding Hood.'

I slammed the door. At least, I thought, they'll have a topic of conversation if the film's no good. I returned to *The Last September* and the remains of my yogurt.

I was behaving like my sister Rosie. I thought of her dotty and irrational behaviour when ensnared by what she called love – usually infatuation for some totally unsuitable nerd . . . usually of the sporting variety. She, of course, ended by making Mother happy and marrying a barrister, who is rising at speed and confines his sporting activities to some mild tennis and sailing on Thursday evenings and Saturdays from the Royal Irish Yacht Club in Dun Laoghaire.

Why do we always feel we have to make our mothers happy? That's just a passing thought. I will not dwell on it now. I will gather together my papers and go and talk about *The Last September* and the decay of the Big House in Ireland. Yawn. By the way, I must remember always that Rosie is a happy person. She has found a place for herself in the Scheme of Things. My major problem being that I don't believe that there is a Scheme of Things.

To get back to brass tacks.

After the lecture I walked quite fast along the corridor towards my office, almost ran in fact, except that I thought that to run would lay me open to ribald comments from my colleagues.

What did I have time to do? What did I need to do? Everything.

Tidy the flat.

Wash the dishes.

Make the bed.

Buy some flowers . . . food.

Have a bath.

Pick up the clothes from my bedroom floor. (Slut.)

Wash my hair.

Scrape my face off and put a new one on, if only, if only.

An endless list with virtually no achievement potential. That thought made me smile. No time for smiling, I said to myself. Get out of this place as quickly as possible. But try and walk with decorum. Footsteps approached me.

'Hello,' he said. 'What's the rush?'

'You?'

'Sure is.' He opened his arms for me, but I swerved to the right and managed to open the door of my office before he touched me. I pulled him inside.

'We must never do that again,' he said. Then he kissed me.

'What?' I asked, when I had disentangled myself and picked all my papers up from the floor.

'Leave each other.'

'I didn't leave you. You abandoned me.'

'Yes.'

'For ten days. No word.'

'Yes. Forgive me.'

He pulled me so hard against him that I could barely breathe.

'Forgive me.'

'Why should I?'

'Forgive me.'

I shook my head.

'Darling, I told you I would be away for a week.'

'No word.'

'I couldn't. I promise you. She was like a bird of prey, watching me all the time. I am a coward, I know I am. Forgive me for my cowardice at least.'

'Spend tonight with me.'

He let go of me and took a couple of steps towards the window. 'There's nothing I'd like more . . .'

Then why not? I thought in my head. Why fucking not?

'Yes. I'll do that.' He turned and threw his arms around me again and we danced a little dance. 'Yes. I'll have to run now though. I'll be back in about an hour. I really will.' He kissed the side of my neck and was away out the door before I could say a word.

Gioir.

I find I get so tired when I write about him. The truth makes my hands heavy.

I ask myself why I still see our meetings touched by this heightened light, like the sun in the street earlier, making plain ordinary objects – houses, trees, motor cars – seem unearthly for a few moments, only for a few moments, and then reality asserts itself again. I know that when I come to write this book, breathe life into my notes, that I will have to address the realities of my relationship with James. I cannot believe that I cut myself off wantonly from life and lived for week after week in this bamboozlement of romantic love.

I must stop writing *gioir,* for a start.

Anyway it was pissing rain when I got out into the street, big drops that burst when they hit you and seemed to bounce up from the pavement, so that you were being attacked by water from all directions. I ran and skidded and had to wait impatiently at each red light, so by the time I reached the safety of my own front door I was drenched. I had bought neither flowers nor food and I had a slight nagging pain near the base of my back. I opened the glass door to the garden and let the fresh damp air clear out the stuffiness. I put clean sheets on the bed and tidied up the bathroom and then stepped into the shower and let the hot water run at full force down over my head and shoulders, beating away anxiety.

It was almost two hours before he arrived and I sat by the open door and listened to the fragments of people's lives. Children squabble, someone rather unwillingly practises scales on a piano, windows open, windows shut, a kettle screeches, there is laughter, a sudden riff from a drummer high up on the top floor, and the pigeons peck on the ground under the ginkgo. It is as clear in my head now as it was then: I can even get the whiff of the damp air in my nose as I write.

After about an hour and a half I began to think that he wasn't coming; that he had told his mother he was spending the night away from home and that she had vaporised him. I sat by the open door and looked out into the garden and wished yet again that I was at home.

I never even heard the creak of the door or his steps as he

crossed the room. The first inkling I had of his arrival was the weight of his hands on my shoulders and his warm voice murmuring into my ear. 'Clara. Clara.'

How long ago?

Almost a year, but still as I tap out my name, I can hear his voice, I can feel the heat that ran through my whole body. I never liked my name before that moment, but I loved it that evening as he spoke it over and over again.

I think this is a good moment to stop.

Unlike Lar, I wish to forget. I would like in ten years' time to be able to look at these pages and laugh.

Five years.

One year.

That's better.

clllm.

You may now switch off.

✻ ✻ ✻

He found the doctor an easy man to talk to. Non-judgemental. Still.

A stranger.

That was important. How easy it is to talk to a stranger, as long as they remain still. If they just breathe in and out, in and out. Nod briefly, smile from time to time.

The doctor sat across the table leaning slightly forward, his chin propped on his right hand.

I suppose, thought Lar, he does this every day, leans towards his patients like this, listening with care until they have finished whatever it is they want to tell him.

He told him everything: about their house above the sea and the steps going down to the sandy bay, about the shed where her pictures were stacked with their faces to the wall, like children being punished. He told him about his mother who always wore grey and his father, about being careful, always being careful and the tensions that caused inside your head. 'Everyone pretends we have been living a normal life. Everyone pretends to understand. Everyone pretends that if this happened or that happened we would all love each other and be in some way translated into paradise.'

He stopped and looked across the table at the doctor. 'Of course,' he said, 'I merely mean some form of normality. Life without hate. Or maybe that is not possible.'

The doctor said nothing.

Lar sighed. 'My mother believes that if we suffer with dignity and resignation in this life, we will be rewarded in the next.'

The doctor spoke for the first time.

'A lot of people are comforted by such thoughts. I presume they make life a little more bearable than it otherwise might be. I do hope so.'

He stood up abruptly.

'I have to go. I don't want her to have reason to . . . ah . . . shout at me again. Finding me still here might upset her. You should go home, Lar. This is not the place for you.' He tapped on the table almost angrily as he spoke and Lar found it hard to decide whether he meant this room or this city. 'I don't mean to sound uncivil but I do think that you should telephone to your mother right away and tell her that you are coming home. I'm sure it will give her comfort. Let her tidy up your house for you.

Give her that bit of satisfaction. I am sure that . . .' He stopped. 'I am sorry,' he said after a moment. 'Forgive me. I really should not be interfering.' He turned and left the room, closing the door quietly behind him.

Lar moved over to the window and watched him walk slowly down the path to the gate, where he stood for a moment, head slightly bowed with his hand on the latch. The wind lifted a little lock of his hair and stretched it sideways.

Lar picked up the telephone and dialled his parents' number. The doctor opened the gate and went out into the street; he turned left and disappeared from Lar's sight.

'Hello.'

'Mum.'

'Laurence! It's so good to hear your voice, son. We were so worried after your call the other day. Your father's not in at the moment. He's just gone for a little walk. The rain eased off and he thought . . . Where are you? Are you still in Dublin? Are you all right, son? I'm so sorry your father isn't here.'

'Give me a chance to speak, Mum, for heaven's sake. It's you I want to talk to anyway. I'll have all the time in the world to talk to Dad when I get home.'

'You're coming . . . oh, son. Oh.'

'Don't cry. Don't cry, Mum, otherwise I'll have to ring off. This is a friend's phone and I can't be wasting her money on listening to you bawling.'

She gave a little laugh. 'You sound more like your old self. If you give me your number I can get your father to—'

'No. I'll be home tomorrow – before dark, I hope. I wondered if I could ask you to do something for me.'

'Anything.'

'Would you have a look at the house? I just marched out of it. Maybe if you could put the heat on, open a window or so, get me in some milk and bread — that sort of thing. Don't kill yourself. I'm sorry to be a bother.'

'It's no bother.' She whispered the words almost as if she were afraid that he would change his mind.

'Thanks. Yes, Look, Mum . . . I have to say a lot of things and I may not get round to saying them.'

'It's all right, Laurence. Just come home — that's all we want. I'll leave the lights on in your house for you. I wouldn't want you to be going into a dark house. If you want to come on up to us, do that, but suit yourself. I'll see you soon. You can say as much or as little as you want. It's a long enough drive home. Take it easy.'

'Yes. Tell Dad I'm sorry.'

'You can tell him that yourself. It's good to hear your voice, son. I feel ten years younger. Goodbye for now.'

Slowly he put down the receiver. He looked across the room to Pansy, in her usual place by the Aga. 'I think we'll go home.' She smiled at him.

'Well, glory be.' Clara was standing in the doorway behind him.

'I rang my mother,' he said.

'Where's the doctor?'

'He left about ten minutes ago.'

She came into the room and stood looking slightly distracted. 'He was right,' she said. 'The coffee was disgusting.' She picked up the dirty cups and took them over to the sink. 'So, he talked some sense into you?'

Lar shook his head. 'No. He didn't say anything much at all.'

'That's the way of him. He's a blotting-paper sort of person; he soaks up other people's woes. Come unto me all ye that labour and are heavy laden and I will give you rest. Is that blasphemous? It's very much the nature of that man.'

She emptied the remains of the coffee into the sink and ran the tap for a moment. She put a hand into the splashing water and rubbed it over her face.

'So, you're going back to the war zone.'

'Home. You can be very unhelpful. It's no longer a war zone. Technically we have peace. At this moment.'

'I mean your own personal battlefield. I know that you haven't told me what really happened to Caitlin and the baby . . .'

'Moya,' he murmured.

'Moya. Yes. I don't know why. We all have our reasons for keeping things secret. I haven't told you a damn thing about me either. None of that matters. You're a nice man and,' she smiled at him, 'you have a nice dog. Maybe if we had both come clean to each other we might have fallen into each other's arms and tried to push misery away that way.'

'I . . .'

He felt his face getting red.

'You're . . .'

Her smile became a grin. 'I'm not your cup of tea, I know that. But it's amazing what can happen when you unburden yourself to someone. When you find someone else in the black hole with you, the obvious thing seems to be to reach out to whoever it is. It's never a solution to anything, merely a few moments of oblivion. Fucking for oblivion's sake. My mother would disapprove.'

Indeed she would, he thought. So, of course, would mine. He thought of her stepping out of the house at that moment, carefully pulling the door tight shut behind her, her hands in grey woollen gloves, her coat collar pulled up high against the sharp wind that blew always in the spring.

Clara touched his hand. 'You've gone away,' she said.

'Not far. Only to the Glens of Antrim. Do you think it'll have changed in three weeks?'

'For God's sake, that place up there hasn't changed in three hundred years.'

'You're so full of bloody prejudice.'

'At least I admit it.'

He grimaced. 'What did you say your doctor's name is?' he asked, changing the subject.

' "Doctor". That's what I call him. I've called him that since I was fifteen. I'll probably call him that for ever.'

'He must have a name. Everyone has a name.'

'I always forget. He has such a silly name I expunge it from my mind.'

'More prejudice.'

' "Doctor" suits him fine. You know, I used to think, after Dad died that he might become Mother's toy boy. One of those silly fantasies. She was only fifty and I hated to see her alone. I know that lots of people resent their parents finding new partners, but it would have been really handy to have him factored into our lives. I think we'd all have been pleased. Even Dad from beyond the grave. She would have had him to look after and that would have taken her mind off me.'

He was shocked. He was thinking of his mother, her almost ghostlike fragility. To him she had always been an old woman; the same age now as she had been when he was at school, when he first met Caitlin, when Moya was born. Without really ever thinking about it he had known that she was pure as the Virgin Mary had been pure, his own conception probably immaculate. In other words, he mused somewhat sourly to himself, he had never thought very much about her.

Clara was laughing. 'Have I shocked you? Lookit here, you shouldn't be shocked by me. I just say these things off the top of my head. I didn't really mean that. I invented it at that moment. Just thought of it then. I do that all the time. Instant stories. All you're meant to do is laugh.'

'I'm not very good at laughing. I'm not good at discovering what is a joke and what is not. Caitlin pointed that out to me many times.'

'His name is Ivan.' Her voice was gentle. 'Such a name to burden any child with. I refuse to call anyone Ivan, unless of course they're Russian. Yes. I'd have to do it then. Wouldn't I?'

He smiled nervously. 'You do have funny notions.'

'So when do you intend to go?'

'I think I'll wait until tomorrow morning, if that's all right with you. I'd like to get away early – give Pansy a run and then set out. Then I can take my time. Stop here and there, let the dog stretch her legs. I told my mother I'd be home before dark.'

'I'm sure you're doing the right thing.'

'I don't really have much alternative. That's what I've come up with in the last few days. I have to thank you for that. If I'd stayed over in the other place, God knows what I would have come up with.'

He looked at her in silence for a long time. 'Have you any tidy clothes?' he asked finally.

'Of course I have. You don't think I've spent all my life looking post-operative, do you? Looking like a hag?'

'I suppose not.' He sounded dubious.

'Any reason?'

'Well, it's back to food again. I just thought that maybe you'd come out and have a meal with me, somewhere a bit posh. A sort of reconciliatory meal . . . also a thank you.' He smiled at her; it was that charming smile that she had noticed before. 'I'd like to thank you and I don't suppose an invitation to the Glens of Antrim would be acceptable.'

She shook her head. 'Yeah,' she said. 'I can dig out some tidy clothes. I can surprise you.'

'Good. Well, back you go to your computer. Maybe I will surprise you too.'

The small hours

The Gingerbread Woman

(continued)

Of course he didn't stay the night.

I thought that he was going to. I finally fell asleep with his arms around me, feeling as I drifted into dreamless darkness, that some threshold had been crossed, that for the first time in my restless life I was heading for a calm happiness that I had never known before.

I was so deeply and confidently asleep that I never stirred when he left the bed. It was the sound of running water that woke me. I lay in our warmth with my eyes tight shut listening to the sounds of someone else living in my life and waiting for him to come back into the bed. The sounds changed. Soft bumpings and rustlings made me open my eyes; it was still dark, but the light from the street laid bars of silver across the floor. He was standing on one foot pulling on a sock.

I sat up.

'What are you doing?'

'I have to go.' He whispered the words and groped around for his trousers.

I switched on the light.

'You'll see better with the light on.'

I looked at my watch. It was ten to two.

'I have to be at the office when the Tokyo Exchange opens. It's important.'

He still whispered. I wondered to myself why was it that people whisper in the dark even when there is no need to. My voice sounded very loud when I spoke. Maybe of course it was very loud; maybe I was shouting at him, though I didn't intend to.

'It's ten to two. Unless of course the watch you gave me is wrong.'

He gave a little laugh as he zipped up his pants. 'Those watches never go wrong. They're hours ahead of us in Japan. Look, darling, I'm sorry. I didn't mean to wake you. I thought I could just slip out without . . .'

'Thanks. You're so thoughtful.'

'I was going to ring you at some reasonable time and explain. Something came up last night – I'm sorry. It's all part of the money game. You want to be rich and powerful, you've got to be prepared to play the game this way.' He was almost gabbling, anxious to be away. He flicked at his hair with a comb and pulled on his jacket. I heard a cab draw up outside the house. He heard it too. I saw that on his face.

'Don't be cross. I love you.' He blew me a kiss. 'Go back to sleep, my darling. I'll call you.'

Then he was gone. After a few moments I heard the cab door slam and it drove off.

Of course I never went back to sleep.

I wondered about the niggling pain in my back.

I wondered why he didn't tell me things that I really ought to know.

Was this something to do with my personality or his?

Did he see in me some capability for anger, throwing things, petulant violence? I didn't see myself like that in any way.

Was he perhaps a man who liked to keep information to himself, even to the point of lying to the people he loved and trusted?

How well did I know him?

Well, well, well, a voice in my head shouted.

Don't fool yourself, came a warning whisper. I wondered what my mother would be saying to me if she were here. That was when I should have fallen asleep, but I didn't.

The phone rang at a quarter past seven. 'Did I wake you?' he asked.

'No. I've been awake since ten to two.'

'I am always having to ask you to forgive me.'

I didn't reply to that, there seemed no need.

'This evening.' His voice was tentative. 'Clara, I want to see you this evening. May I?'

'They're showing *Les Enfants du Paradis* at the local cinema. I want to see that. That's where I should have been last night only you turned up. Have you ever seen it?'

'No.'

'It's a dream film. Let's go to that and then eat out afterwards. That's what I'd like to do. Like I've said before, I want to do something normal with you. A lot of normal things.'

He didn't speak

'James K'van,' I said. 'Are you still there?'

'I'm here. I can't stay the night. My mother's back again. So if we went to the movies and then ate out, we couldn't . . . we wouldn't have time to . . .'

'There are other things that can be enjoyed – like talking and meeting people, going places together and really getting to know each other. We seem to have forgotten all about those things.'

'Have you stopped loving me?'

I laughed. 'No. By no means.'

'I was away too long, I realise that now. I have let you slip through my fingers.'

'What a cod you are.'

'What does that mean?'

'Sorry . . . Irishspeak. I'll translate for you the next time I see you.'

A confused sound of voices reached my ear and then a door slammed.

'Where are you?' I asked.

'Having breakfast. We had no dinner last night, remember? I have to have breakfast. It's a noisy coffee-house just down the street from the office. I have to go, my darling. Yes. Seven o'clock will suit me fine. We will do as you suggested. Goodbye.' He put the receiver down.

Have I won a battle or lost it? I wondered.

Why bother wondering?

I fell asleep and had to rush to get to work on time.

Les Enfants du Paradis

The tragic white clown face of Barrault has always remained in my mind since the first time I saw the film at the age of eighteen, on a holiday in London. Now it has more poignance than ever before, as it was standing by a blown-up picture of the clown, arms outstretched, head drooping comically to one side, and tears swelling from his eyes, that the bubble of unreality in which I had been living burst.

Big Bang.

I can laugh now. I can make jokes about it now. I don't want to see that lovely film though for years to come; I don't want to cry as I watch it for all the wrong reasons.

He held my hand, from time to time raising it to his mouth and kissing each knuckle. His fingers held me tight, just as if, I believed at that moment, he never wanted to let me go. When the film was over he turned me towards him and wiped the tears from my cheeks with his fingers and then we went out into the street. We stood for a moment beside the poster, and the crowd leaving the cinema gently buffeted us as they passed.

'So?' I asked him. 'What do you think?'

'Thank you,' he said. 'Give me a list of great movies like that and we will go and see them all. We will spend the rest of our lives going to see them. Thank—'

'Hi, James. *Quelle surprise*. Didn't know you ever went to the movies. How are things with you?'

James let go of my hand. He looked resigned, as if this was something that he knew was going to happen sometime.

'Richard! Good to see you. It's been ages.'

Richard stuck his hand out towards me. 'Richard Hayes,' he said.

I shook his hand. I was about to tell him my name, but he spoke again.

'How about we go find a drink?'

James shook his head. 'Sorry, I have to dash. Another time, yeah? We must get together soon.'

'How are Carla and the kids? Betsy and I were saying just the other day that you must come down and spend a weekend in Long Island with us. We have the house all fixed up now. It looks terrific. I'll get Betsy to give Carla a call.'

'Great, do that. We'll look forward to that.'

We all stood for a moment not quite sure which way we should all turn, then with a little wave of his hand the Richard person turned right and ran across the road. He couldn't wait, I decided, to get home to tell Betsy, but maybe no; maybe there was a fraternal instinct that would get to work here. You scratch my back, buddy, and I'll . . .

James took my arm just above the elbow. I pulled away from him.

'How about we go find a drink?' I sneered in my best New York voice.

I set off along the street heading for the sort of bar he had probably never been into in his life – preferably Irish, I thought, filled with green lights and shamrocks, flashing signs for Guinness and collecting boxes for Noraid on the counter. The sort of bar that I normally wouldn't be seen dead in. A drum was beating in my head and the street, cars and lights and sidewalk and people passing were splintered and silvered by the tears that gathered behind my eyes. I didn't bloody want to cry. I was almost running. I bit at the inside of my mouth to inhibit the tears.

I could hear his feet behind me.

Once he called my name.

'Clara!'

I just scurried on.

Where is your dignity? a voice in my head asked me.

Fuck dignity.

I got the smell of beer and turned into a brown doorway. It was warm and horrible inside and dark. I liked the dark. A woman's voice wailed about green fields and fiddles played. I pushed my way to the bar, pulled my purse out of my pocket and fumbled in it for money. A pink-faced young man with curly hair smiled at me from the other side of the bar.

'What'll it be?'

'A pint of Guinness and a large Jameson, please.'

He nodded. I took out some notes and put them on the bar. James reached over my shoulder and picked them up and shoved them back into my hand.

'Clara. This is a grim place. Let's go somewhere quiet. Somewhere we can talk.'

I put the notes back on the bar and nodded at the young man. He wiggled his eyebrows at me, sensing trouble.

'I can talk here,' I said.

'I can't even think . . .'

'Well, you're going to have to try because this is where I'm staying.'

The young man put the glass of whiskey down on the counter and shoved a jug of water along the bar towards me.

'There's a table over there,' he said. 'I'll bring the Guinness when it's pulled.'

'Thanks.'

I decided to drink the whiskey neat. I picked up the glass and headed for a small table by the wall.

'Get yourself a drink,' I said to James. 'These are both for me.' I put the glass on the table and sat down. I had seldom drunk whiskey in my life and I hated Guinness.

James stood looking down at me.

'Sit,' I said, as one would to a dog. After a moment he sat.

I took a sip from the glass.

'OK,' I said. 'Shoot.'

For a moment I was quite enjoying myself, but I knew it wouldn't last long. I took a larger sip. He didn't seem to know the meaning of the word. The barman arrived with my Guinness at that moment and put the glass carefully on a mat that had *Harp Lager* written across it. He put my change down beside the glass.

'Thanks,' I said. 'Keep that. It'll go towards your ticket home.'

'I have my ticket home, but ta all the same.' He put the coins in his pocket. 'Can I get you anything, sir?' He smiled towards James.

'No.'

The barman wiggled his eyebrows at me again and left us. Probably, I thought, making more than I do teaching people about Elizabeth Bowen. Morose thought.

'Clara . . .'

'Let's get something straight. Who is this Carla? Your sister? You never told me you had a sister. Your mother? Your mother's called Carla. Isn't it odd that if you just shove the letters round a bit you get Clara. Carla's a bit more glamorous really. Clara's rather old-fashioned, lumpy. Yes, it's a lumpy name. Maybe I'll change it to Carla.' I took another drink and leant towards him. I spoke in a loud whisper. 'Who the fuck is Carla?'

'My wife.' He held his hand up like a policeman. 'Don't say anything. Let me explain.'

'Sure. Go ahead, explain.'

'Carla is my wife.'

'I've got that.'

'We've been . . . well, not exactly separated, but not exactly together for some time now. We married too young, just out of college, and recently things began to fall apart. We've changed so much. We're not the same people that we were when we married. It's like strangers living in the same house.'

'She doesn't understand you,' I suggested.

He looked cross. 'Carla . . . I mean Clara . . . let's not have jokes about this. It's too serious. I love you. You have to believe me.'

'What about your poor demented mummy?'

'Unh?'

'Tell me all about her. Tell me for instance the truth about her. Do you have a mummy?'

'Of course I do. She's—'

'Crazed with grief.'

'Well, no, she's recovered. Although it took a long time. She was fragile for an age, just like I said. Really dependent and clinging, after my father died. But . . . she's in Connecticut. She's, ah, OK now. Fine. Yes. She did go through a bad patch though. Believe me. Look, darling, I'm truly sorry. I got caught in a sort of web . . . a maze of lies. I have been so upset about it all. So upset about the things I was saying to you.'

'I've noticed.'

'Everything will be all right now. Different. I promise.' He stretched his hand across the table, hoping to find mine. I picked up the whiskey glass and held it against my chest, like a shield, held tight in my laced fingers.

'And the children. Tell me about them.'

'Three. Maria, Julia and Anna.'

It was like getting treacle from a well. 'Ages?'

'Ten, six and . . . ah . . . two months.'

'Two months!'

'Well, nearly.'

'You mean to say that your wife has had a baby since you and

I . . . since . . . This woman with whom you do not really live? You mean to say that?'

'I mean to say,' he leant towards me, his voice low and very controlled, 'that I have a wife with whom I live; sometimes we have friendly relations, most of the time we do not. I do not hate her. I do not love her, but I live with her. I love my children. I love you. I have told you that and you must believe it. I have been very, very foolish, Clara. I realise that now. If this is causing you pain, I can only say how sorry I am. They were well-intentioned lies I told you.'

'I like that. I like well-intentioned lies. I must remember that.'

'Don't fool about, Clara. Now you know the truth we can begin to put our relationship on a more stable footing.'

'A what?'

'Work out a pattern.'

I was trembling all over; I was literally shaking in my shoes. I wondered if I was going to be able to stand up. Quickly I swallowed the rest of the whiskey and put the glass on the table. I twisted my hands tightly together, hurting my fingers as I squeezed and pressed. The whiskey was burning my throat.

'And anagram . . .?'

He looked puzzled. 'An — a — gram. My anagram, my alter ego, my shadow — does she know about me? I am her anagram. Carla — Clara. Isn't that delightful? Will she find it delightful and join us in creating a pattern?'

'Don't be silly, Clara. Finish your drink, darling, and let's go somewhere else.'

I stood up slowly and reached out for the pint of Guinness.

I had at last discovered the purpose of Guinness, I thought to myself as I poured it quite slowly, or so it seemed to me, over his head.

'Hey!'

The brown liquid foamed down over his face, into his eyes and ears and down his neck. His pale blue Brooks Brothers' shirt became brown, his tie was streaked with the liquid. It ran round the collar of his jacket and then over his shoulders. A pint is quite a lot of liquid. I was hoping that it would penetrate through all his clothes to his pale golden skin.

'Explain that to the anagram,' I said and left the bar.

The barman shouted something after me that sounded like, 'That's the stuff to give the troops.' But I wouldn't swear to it.

I don't remember getting home, dodging through the people and the traffic, along Bleecker and across the Avenue of the Americas, but I eventually found myself on my doorstep. My eyes were not focusing and my hands were shaking. I sat down on the step and emptied my bag out onto the ground beside me, hoping to find my key. I put my head in my hands and began to cry. Like a romantic fool I sat hunched on the step and wept; tears spread out from under my hands and over my chin. I tasted the salt in my mouth, the collar of my shirt was wet, my nose ran slime. That was too much. I groped on the ground beside me for a tissue. I had no luck, but at least I found my keys. I wiped my face on my sleeve, shoved my rubbish back into my bag and stood up.

That was when a savage pain in my back suddenly assaulted me and I had to hold onto the railing for a moment before I was able to move. I could hear the telephone in my bedroom ringing.

I was glad I wasn't there to answer it. After a few minutes the pain eased and I went into the house. The telephone was still ringing as I let myself in the door of my apartment. I hobbled across the room and picked up the receiver.

'Fuck off!' I yelled into it, hoping to burst his eardrum. I slammed the receiver down again and pulled the plug out of the wall. I went into the bathroom and washed my face. I looked horrible both before and after washing. In the cabinet over the basin was a box of Neurofen, unopened; I was not a pill popper and had just brought it with me in case of emergencies. This seemed to me to be an emergency. I took four. I was not contemplating suicide, merely oblivion for a while. I drank a glass of water and went and lay down fully dressed on my bed.

I wanted my mother.

＊   ＊   ＊

They both surprised each other.

She had taken from her press a dark cinnamon skirt and long jacket that she had bought in New York and hung them on the back of her door to give them an airing, also in the hope that the creases would disappear without her having to iron them.

I have so many hideous lumps and bumps, she thought as she looked at herself in the mirror after her bath, all nowadays in the wrong places, all strange colours, all pretty bloody unattractive. But what does it matter? This is not a date you're going on. It's just dinner with a passing acquaintance. A very passing acquaintance, in fact almost past.

She put a lot of eye make-up on and painted her mouth dark red. 'OK, Queen of the Vampires.' She grinned at herself in the glass, clamped the large gold watch round her wrist and went to look for Lar.

He had been at the ironing board, she thought. His shirt was neat, the cuffs just showing beneath the sleeves of a brown tweed jacket, a sober tie knotted in a tight old-fashioned knot just under the jut of his Adam's apple. Not cool, but polished and smelling faintly of aftershave. She wondered if he had gone out during the afternoon and bought that.

He was sitting watching the news and Pansy sat beside him, her head on his knee, watching his face with care as if she needed to read his thoughts.

'Da-daaa!'

Clara posed by the door, one hand on the frame, the other on her hip.

He jumped to his feet. He looked startled by her appearance, as if, she thought, he had already moved out of her life and was expecting to see some totally different person.

'Oh, hello,' he stammered. 'Great, you look great.' He plunged a hand into a pocket and rattled some coins. He cleared his throat, laughed suddenly. 'You certainly don't look post-operative.'

She was pleased that he felt like making a joke and laughed too. 'How about a glass of wine before we go? Where are we going anyway?'

'I bought a bottle of champagne – it's in the fridge. Will I open that? I've ordered a taxi.'

'My word, we are pushing out the boat.' She regretted having said that and put out her hand towards him. 'I'm sorry. I'd love some champagne. It is the most medicinal of all drinks, and no matter how you say I look, I am still in need of medication.'

He reached out and touched her hand briefly. He went into the kitchen and she listened to him opening and closing doors. I don't really like this man, she thought, and yet here I am all dollied up and prepared to spend an evening in flirtatious conversation with him — or that's the way things seem to be moving. Pop the champagne cork and flirtation seems to be in the air.

Effervescence.

Perhaps that is all there is to me. A few bubbles here, a few there; gone in a flash, leaving no memory. Oh, I expect a few students will remember some of the rubbish I have churned out in my life, about Elizabeth Bowen, Kate O'Brien, formidable ladies, Edna O'Brien, Iris Murdoch, none of them effervescent, vanishing women. God, I need that champagne, and quick, before I change my mind about this outing and opt to spend the evening in front of the telly.

'Hey!' He was standing in front of her, a full glass in each hand.

'You do slip away.' He offered her a glass.

'Thank you.' She took the glass from his hand.

Bubbles rose and rose to the top. She held it up, towards him.

'The man from North Antrim.'

'The Gingerbread Woman.'

She gave a little gasp as he said those words. 'How odd. Why do you call me that?'

'I don't know. That's what you look like, all dressed up in those clothes. You look good. Don't be offended.'

'I'm not. Just a bit bemused. You see, it's what I'm going to call this book I may be writing.' She lifted the glass to her lips and the bubbles rose and rose into her mouth. She tilted her head back and the liquid bubbled down her throat. The glass was empty. She held it out towards him.

He frowned.

'That bottle cost twenty-five quid.'

'Worth every penny.'

'We should savour it.'

'I am, believe me. I'd like to savour some more.'

He went back into the kitchen to get the bottle.

'A great way to get rid of money,' she called after him. 'You never answered my question.'

'What was that?' He came back and poured more bubbles into her waiting glass.

'Just about where we're having dinner.'

For a moment he said nothing. Then he put the bottle down on the table.

'It's a place Caitlin always wanted to go. She'd heard about it, met the odd person who'd been there. She always had a fancy for me to take her there. I thought . . .'

'Look – this isn't a very good idea.'

'I thought,' he raised his voice slightly, 'that she would like me to take you there. You've been so kind. I know she would like me to do that.'

'Where is this place? What is it called?'

'It's in that hotel owned by U2.'

'The Clarence? You're mad, man. It costs an arm and a leg. This is . . .'

'I've booked us a table.'

She was about to say 'ridiculous', but changed her mind. '. . . terribly kind. Terribly, extravagantly kind.'

'She would . . .' He stopped. He sipped at his wine. 'It's my pleasure,' he said.

She smiled at him.

Her smile made him think of bodies touching and the smell he had got from her pillow of tangled hair and warmth.

I'm going to tell her the truth tonight, he thought. To hell with her mother. I'm going to sit in that restaurant and with Caitlin at my shoulder, I will tell her everything. About love and hate and despair and the blackness that has covered my life for two years, and maybe she will touch me and where her fingers lie the blackness will peel away like a tired skin. Yes, I will do that.

He wanted to go now, this minute, but she was still standing there, glass in hand, still smiling towards him and there was no taxi and he didn't know how to fill in this waiting time until he had her across the table imprisoned in the restaurant, so he just smiled back at her and said, 'Yes, my pleasure.'

The doorbell rang and Pansy barked, one sharp loud bark.

'The taxi?' suggested Clara, dipping her head down again towards her glass. Lar nodded and left the room. Pansy padded after him towards the hall door.

Clara wondered whether another quick fill-up would be in order or not and had just decided that there would be no harm in it when the doctor came into the room.

'I have to talk to you,' he said.

She waved a hand towards the bottle. 'Have a glass of champagne. Lar, get him a glass. We're going out. There's a taxi.'

'No, thanks. No drink.' He turned to Lar. 'Would you mind leaving us? I have something I want to say to Clara.'

'No,' said Clara. 'We're going out. Look at me. When did you last see me all dressed up? Dressed to kill.' She laughed suddenly. 'Though, I do have to say, I don't intend to kill anyone this evening. We're having a celebration and you mustn't interrupt, unless it's something urgent. It's not anything to do with Mother, is it? You're not going to spring something on me about her?'

'No. Clara, please calm down. It's nothing to do with your mother. Or any of the others.'

Out in the street the taxi hooted.

'The taxi,' said Lar.

Clara put her glass on the table. 'It's OK, Lar. We're going. You go on out – I'll be after you in a tick.' She waited until he had left the house, leaving the door wide open and a little wind rippling the rug in the hall.

'You just came most untimely, Doctor. I'm sorry if I was rude, but he's made all these arrangements – such *unlikely* arrangements, I have to concentrate my thoughts on him. I have to give all the appearances of enjoying my evening. You must admit I've made an effort. Please admire me.' She stood hands out with a slight smile on her face.

'I admire you.'

'So, if it's something awful about the state of my health, can it wait till tomorrow?'

'Let me reassure you it is nothing like that. It is something purely personal.'

He looked her up and down.

'I do so admire you, Clara. Well, you'd better be off. Enjoy your evening. Maybe we'll talk tomorrow. Maybe there won't be time or place for what I have to say. Maybe I'll go back down to Oughterard, finish my holiday. Maybe . . . Clara.'

She put her hand on his shoulder. 'You look tired. Stay here a while. Have some medicinal champagne, put your feet up, watch telly, talk to the dog, make yourself at home. No one can bother you here.'

She was gone out of the door, pulling it closed behind her, before he had time to reply.

✳   ✳   ✳

Midnight.

What a weirdo evening that was.

Safely home and sitting at my work table.

Recollecting.

Recollecting is also weird.

I am only thinking now; I haven't yet got my fingers working on the keyboard. That will be recollection of a different nature. Lar has taken the dog for a walk.

There was no sign of the doctor when we arrived home. I had been anxious on the way back, thinking he might still be here, waiting and hungry to unburden himself of whatever it was that had been troubling him. I don't like to see him troubled. But it wouldn't have suited me at all to find him here as I have tonight earmarked for getting these painful notes finished, off my chest, out of my hair.

Will I then feel purged? I shouldn't think so. But maybe by the time I wake up tomorrow morning I may feel that I have salvaged something from the wreck.

That's all we can do, really. Keep salvaging.

But before I open up, I'd like to clear my head of the evening's conversation – well, monologue really. I was not allowed to speak, not a word, except to order my meal. I was hardly allowed to eat. Lar became more and more like the ancient mariner, staring across the table, on and on telling me this story that I didn't want to hear, but that he insisted I *had* to hear. I had to share eye contact with him, and if I dropped my eyes to my plate or let them wander round the high, gaunt room he would grab my hand and hold it painfully tight until my eyes returned once more to his face. I didn't want to hear his story. I wanted to put my fingers in my ears and close my eyes, so that I couldn't even see his mouth opening and closing. On and on.

Now my head is filled with his story, Caitlin's story. The story of where hate leads you. Down a grotesque path that ends with the little nursery song that he sang in a low voice, leaning towards me across the table covered with expensive glasses, linen, china. 'Old Macdonald had a farm, ee.i.ee.i.o.'

Very low his voice was as he sang, almost a raging whisper.

'And on that farm he had a pig . . .'

I feel now as if his eyes had left scorchmarks on my face, as if the hand he held so tight had been burned by the heat of his fingers and his anger.

Slowly he released his grip and we were at the side of their grave, Caitlin and the little girl. He was wearing his clean shirt and his mother was beside him, dressed from head to toe in grey, holding his arm so that he couldn't escape. I felt the cold and the sorrow by that grave and he became silent and let go my hand and looked down at the table.

'I'm sorry,' he said.

All I could do was nod my head.

He asked for the bill.

I disliked him.

There are times I really despise myself.

I also had the oddest feeling, as I watched him deal with credit card and tips that he was making some kind of play for me. I disliked him even more at that moment.

Sitting here now trying to clear my head for work, I think my imagination must have been working overtime.

He sat very close to me in the taxi on the way home and neither of us spoke.

Pansy greeted us ecstatically. He picked up her lead from the table by the door.

'Goodnight,' I said to him. 'I will be working when you come back. Thank you very much and . . . and I hope I've been some sort of help to you.'

I leant forward and gave him a kiss on the cheek.

'I hope that one day you will be happy again. It is possible.' And I came in here and shut the door.

I hope never to see him again.

Another strange thought has come into my mind, that maybe one day I may use his story; steal it from him. Yes. Maybe he gave me more than I can at this moment handle, something to ferment and foment in the dark cavities of the brain.

cccclllllmmm.

There we go.

The screen is lighting up. Terse but friendly messages pass across it, leaving a lovely inviting empty space. I wonder again why I never recognised the exciting possibilities of the empty page before.

Closed mind.

The Gingerbread Woman

(continued)

When I woke up the next morning I felt like death. Whiskey, pills and sorrow sat on my chest and I could barely move. The pain down at the base of my spine was a dull nag. No matter what had happened in my life, I had to go to work so I dragged myself out of bed and into the shower.

I met Sophie in the corridor outside my room.

'Your phone has been ringing for the last twenty minutes,' she said.

I nodded wearily. 'Sorry.'

'You're looking like hell. Are you ill? The grippe or something?'

'No. You were right about the man.' As I opened the door the phone started to ring again. 'Wife. Three kids. Lying turd.'

'Oh God, I'm sorry, Clara. I just had this feeling. Take the day off. We'll manage. Go home and beat your brains out. Is that the rat?' She gestured towards the phone.

'I suppose.'

She crossed the room and picked up the receiver. 'Who is this? No, she's not here. No, she won't be in today. Or tomorrow.

In fact, I think as far as you're concerned she'll never be in again. And goodbye to you too.' She put the phone down. 'Sounds nice. Very Upper East Side. Personally I like them a bit more squalid.'

I laughed a little.

'Go home,' she said.

'No. I'd rather work.'

'We'll lunch,' she promised and went back into her own room.

When we returned after lunch, he was outside my door leaning against the wall. He was, as usual, dressed immaculately, neither sight nor smell of Guinness. I unlocked my door. Sophie stood for a moment, her head slightly to one side. I gave her a little wave and she turned towards her own room.

'You know where I am, if you need me.'

'I have nothing to say to you,' I said to him as I opened the door.

'But I have a lot to say to you.'

'You needn't bother. I really don't want to hear anything.' I stood in the half-open doorway and stared at him and I thought how I wanted him to throw his arms around me and tell me it had all been a terrible mistake. His friend had been telling lies. He was free as air and he loved me. Me. Only me. And I would cry on his shoulder and the pain in my back would go and it would be happy ever after for us both. Fuck fairy tales, I said to myself.

'Anything,' I repeated.

'You don't know how miserable I've been. I haven't slept. I haven't been to work.'

'I do hope there won't be a stock-market crash.'

'Clara . . .'

'What did the anagram have to say about the Guinness?
Don't tell me. She doesn't know. You stopped off at the club
and showered and trotted home in your squash gear.'

He went red.

A hit. A palpable hit! I rather hoped that Sophie had her ear
to the keyhole.

'Can we go in?' He moved towards the door.

I shut it quickly. 'No.'

'This is very public.'

'This is as private as it's going to get.'

'I can explain all this mess. If you'll give me a chance.'

'Come to dinner tonight.'

'Darling, I knew you'd—'

'Bring the anagram. You can explain the mess to both of us
at the same time.'

'Be reasonable.'

'I think that's pretty reasonable. Otherwise just fuck off out
of my life.'

'You don't mean that.'

'Want to bet?'

'In a few days . . .'

'Oh, get out of here, James. Haven't I made it quite clear? I
don't want to see you again or hear your voice on the phone or
smell your aftershave. I despise you for being a lying faithless
cad and I despise myself for having fallen in love with
you. Get out. Go and play games with someone your own size.
Go.' I must have been shouting though it didn't seem like it to
me.

'Ssssh,' he said.

'I will not sssh. I don't care who hears me. Just get out now or I'll call security and have you thrown out. And don't come back.'

He turned and walked down the corridor.

'Bastard!' I shouted after him.

I went into my room and shut the door and burst into tears yet again.

After a moment or two the door opened a crack. I looked up. It was Sophie.

'Great,' she said. 'I loved it when you called him a cad. Sooo terribly British.'

'Just piss off,' was all I could say.

That was it really. I never saw him again. I realised too late that I still had his watch and then that I had no means of sending it back to him — no address, no telephone number, not even the name of the firm he worked with. I shall keep it for ever, I thought to myself, a permanent reminder of my folly. I hoped that it had cost him a lot of money.

Of course I had a more permanent reminder as I discovered when I finally made it home in July. I put off going to the doctor for as long as possible.

'You look grim,' my sister Rosie said to me one day. 'I'm sure you're ill.'

'Psychosomatic,' I said to her. 'I'll be fine. Lower back pain is always psychosomatic.'

'Don't say that to Mum or she'll have your life.'

I said nothing to Mother, but I did catch a worried look on her face from time to time when I was with her.

The pain didn't go away. It became more intense and

my energy drained away with a horrible flow of blood and some sort of mucus that caught me by surprise and stained my clothes, exhausted itself and me and then returned after a few days and brought with it a putrid smell that frightened me more than the pain ever had. I felt as if my insides were rotting.

I dragged myself to the doctor and the whole process was set in motion.

'Please don't tell Mother.'

Doctor was sitting at his desk reading the notes from the specialist.

'My dear Clara, I will have to tell your mother that you're going into hospital. I will have to tell her that you are having a hysterectomy. What I don't have to tell your mother is that you have been infected by sleeping with a man suffering from gonorrhoea, and that you stupidly neglected to see a doctor until it was too late to save your womb. That information is no one's business but your own.'

'You do like calling a spade a spade.'

'A spade *is* a spade, you silly woman. Does he know?'

'Who?'

'This man. This father of your infection.'

'No.'

He folded up the papers in front of him and then unfolded them. He smoothed them out and then began to fold them again. 'You should tell him,' he said at last.

'No. I can't do that.'

'Why not?'

'I just can't, Doctor. Please don't bully me.'

He sighed. 'Don't be melodramatic, Clara. He's probably busy infecting other women.'

'Probably,' I said. 'That's pretty likely.'

I thought of poor old anagram.

Not for long.

She had her three lovely little girls, I thought. She was one of the lucky ones.

He was talking. He was saying something like, 'You know what this means, don't you, Clara? It will take you a long time to come to terms with the implications of this operation, but the world won't come to an end' — all that sort of stuff, and all the time he was speaking he folded and unfolded the papers in front of him. My papers.

I was crying.

Again, again. More tears.

I never knew it was possible to manufacture so many tears, nor so much of that bloody gluk that was seeping out of me as I cried. He came round to me and stood beside me, not touching me, just standing there quite still. I could hear his quiet breathing. He took a handkerchief from his pocket and held it out in front of me. I took it and mopped at my face.

'Please don't tell Mother.'

He took my hand and held it rather as if he were taking my pulse. 'Clara, I promise you I will not tell your mother anything that has to do with your personal life. She will of course surmise and she's not stupid. You must make allowances for that.'

I nodded.

'You're in an awful mess but we'll soon have you right.' He

squeezed my hand gently and then let it go. 'I promise you that.'

'I expect you say that to all the girls.'

'Sometimes it isn't possible,' he said. I suppose he thought that was comforting.

I never tried to get in touch with James. I expect I could have if I had made the effort, but the effort seemed too great. The thought of writing either an accusatory or a pathetic letter to him didn't appeal to me at all.

I think I am my own person.

I realise now that I will have to invent my own immortality.

Perhaps I will take to making jam.

Perhaps I will do something to please my mother.

Perhaps I will go to Oughterard with the doctor. Is that, I wonder, what he was going to ask me?

Perhaps it is time to become a non-fugitive. Sit by a lakeside and watch an aging man fish.

I suppose there are worse ways of spending your life.

I am not dead. I do not hate anyone. Words leap and fall in my head, stumble and rush, fight and chatter, like children I will never have, play and sleep and wake again. I am tired, but I am well. I can laugh again.

Keep salvaging.

It is starting to get light – tiny strips of gold glitter through the trees. The earliest birds are waking and pushing out their soft cries. I will go and make a huge breakfast for that man. Fill him to the brim with food and it will carry him back to North Antrim and his house on the edge of the sea and Caitlin's paintings stacked by the wall in her studio, and I will kiss him goodbye and wave by the gate until his car is down the road and round the corner. He too is his own man. He may not know it yet, but that is his fate. Cccclllllmmm.ccclllmm.

It is safe to switch off your Macintosh.
Go to dark.